7/2003

D1400462

Broken Wagon

NORMAN A. FOX

Broken Wagon

Thorndike Press • Chivers Press
Thorndike, Maine USA Bath, England

This Large Print edition is published by Thorndike Press, USA and by Chivers Press, England.

Published in 2001 in the U.K. by arrangement with Richard Fox.

Published in 2001 in the U.S. by arrangement with Richard Fox.

U.S. Hardcover   0-7862-3238-2 (Western Series Edition)
U.K. Hardcover   0-7540-4533-1 (Chivers Large Print)
U.K. Softcover   0-7540-4534-X (Camden Large Print)

The text of this Large Print edition is unabridged.
Other aspects of the book may vary from the original edition.

Set in 16 pt. Plantin.

Printed in the United States on permanent paper.

British Library Cataloguing in Publication Data available

Library of Congress Cataloging-in-Publication Data

Fox, Norman A., 1911-1960.
    Broken wagon / Norman A. Fox
        p. cm.
    ISBN 0-7862-3238-2 (lg. print : hc : alk. paper)
    1. Newspaper publishing — Fiction. 2. Large type books.
    I. Title.
PS3511.O968 B76 2001
    813'.54—dc21   00-054464

CONTENTS

CHAPTER ONE

Night Stage

By sundown Bowman had let drop the saddle he had carried off the mountain, and clinging only to the saddlebag, he kept to the road he'd reached. He moved briskly enough to fight the cold, resting often to conserve his energy. Only October, but a man could die out here from cold or hunger or the changeless miles — and in him now was the first whisper of panic. This too he fought. "Steady!" he thought, and was surprised when the spoken word beat back at his ears. Around him the hills bulked, high and pine-blanketed, and shortly the moon came out and turned the snow brilliant. The night became vaster in this light and more lonely, more silent.

It was easier to hold to the road in the moonlight, and there had been enough wagon traffic to break ruts he could follow. He kept telling himself another wagon would be coming along any time now, but the silence held and the cold crowded at him. His sheepskin coat was missing one button; his feet felt pinched and leaden in his boots; and the muffler he'd wrapped around his ears, under his hat, kept slipping loose. Presently he sat upon a deadfall log, needing to rest again; and he began to laugh, thinking how secure and warm he'd been in the place he had lately left, thinking of what he carried in his saddlebag and what little good it was to him in these hills to-night. Then he heard the stage.

Mountain air magnified the sounds of creaking thorough-braces and squealing wood; mountain silence carried it across a great distance. The waiting was long; and when the stage did come upon him and hauled to a stop, Bowman was standing in the middle of the road, the saddlebag held out from his body and his right hand raised to show this was no hold-up. Still, the driver had picked up a rifle and held it dead centre on Bowman.

"Sing out, damn you!" the driver called, his voice too shrill and his breath a cloud before his face.

"What do you want?" Bowman asked. "The national anthem?" He supposed he looked big and tough to this driver, and cold had probably pinched his long face into something unpleasant, but he still had his hand up, and his gun was out of sight under his sheepskin. He figured that should be sign enough.

"Crows and Cheyennes are out," the driver said. "Maybe the Gros Ventres and the Piegans, too. War paint everywhere. Man, where you been that you ain't heard?"

"I've heard," Bowman said. "Where you going?"

"We're out of Helena on our way to Broken Wagon," the driver said. He lowered the rifle. "Toss your possibles into the boot and git in. We're late now."

But Bowman still held to his saddlebag as he walked to the door and swung it open. He said over his shoulder, "You'll find my saddle up the road a piece." He had a glimpse of moon-whitened faces at the windows and was struck by the fact on a night bitter as this, the passengers were keeping the curtains rolled up. There were three men inside, two riding forward, one backward; Bowman took the unoccupied half of the latter's seat. The man who made room for him was big and wore a moth-eaten buffalo coat and a hat with a brim too wide for Montana, and he reeked of horses. The stage jolted into motion again,

9

snow crunching under the wheels.

The big man asked, "Now where the hell did you come from?"

"Across the hills," Bowman said. "Horse broke his leg in a windfall, and I had to shoot him."

"Short-cutting with a big fall of snow on the ground and the temperature below zero? You crazy?"

Bowman got it then. This man was afraid; they were all afraid, the three of them and the driver; fear had made the driver jumpy and this one testy. That Indian scare. There had been talk of it at every ranch where Bowman had put in for a meal the last couple of days. The snow in some parts was being broken by the tracks of infantry detachments and the deeper cuts of mountain howitzers and transport wagons as troops converged on the Tongue from Forts Custer and Keogh, Maginnis and McIntosh. Queer doings in this Montana of 1887, this Territory so nearly a state, with telegraph lines everywhere, the Northern Pacific Railway spanning the land, and the Manitoba building in. Queer that the old fear could rise out of years long buried. Ten years this month since Joseph had turned over his rifle to Colonel Miles in the shadow of the Bear Paws and brought the retreat of the Nez Percés to its tragic end. Eleven years since Custer had sought glory and found a grave at the Little Big Horn.

His own concern was not with Indians, Bowman reminded himself. For him there was another danger, one that could grow greater from the suspicions of men. He could feel the curiosity of these three, and he wanted to blunt it. "Crazy?" he said. "Maybe you're right. My notion was that the Indians would keep close to the roads."

"And you saw no Indians?" a man across from him asked. Bowman caught a glimpse of a thin face with tufted eyebrows and a silvery goatee. Here was fear, too, but a thinking man's fear that sought out facts to make the picture brighter or darker as the facts indicated.

Bowman shook his head. "Last I heard, they were around Fort Meade, camped just opposite Custer's battlefield."

"So the newspapers say. It is becoming difficult to separate facts from rumour." The old man sighed. "It seems definite that some Cheyenne hot bloods have joined Sword-Bearer and his Crows. And we're told that Sword-Bearer has sent runners to the Utes in Colorado, to the Shoshones and Piegans, and possibly the

11

Sioux. He's trying to persuade them to a general uprising."

"There can't be over four hundred fighting men in the whole Crow tribe," Bowman said.

"Thirty Gros Ventres crossed the Yellowstone the other night," the old man countered. "General Dudley arrested them and is holding them at his post till the trouble is over. The question is: how many other redskins have decided that now is the time to turn back the clock and start lifting white scalps? Don't you see? They may strike anywhere, any time."

Bowman shrugged.

"My name is Hascomb — Miles Hascomb," the old man said. "We're all acquaintances here. The man beside you is Pete Beale, foreman of the Circle 6 over beyond Broken Wagon, and this gentleman" — he indicated his own silent seat mate — "is known as Faro for his proficiency at that game. I myself am a journalist, the editor and owner of the Broken Wagon *Bugle*, a newspaper so recently established that I dare say you've never heard of it."

"But I have," Bowman said. And because he knew what they were all awaiting, he added, "My name is Neil Bowman."

12

Hascomb said, "It has a familiar ring."

At once wary, Bowman shrugged. "I could be known to all of you. I've polished a few saddles with the seat of my pants, spent some nights at cards, and set type on a small weekly."

Hascomb said with quick interest, "Indeed! I could use a man on my paper."

The silent Faro broke silence. "Not this one, Miles."

Bowman stared at Faro, half angered. In the dimness Faro was a long shadow folded down into the seat, a black-garbed man, his face vague in the gloom. Bowman asked, "What strikes you wrong about me?" His voice came sharper than he'd intended.

Faro shook his head. "I meant nothing personal. I read cards, and I also read men. I merely intended to say that you would not be interested in working for someone else."

"No," Bowman said. "I wouldn't. If I ever work on a newspaper again, it will be my own."

He eased back against the seat, wanting no more of this kind of talk. Next thing, Hascomb would be asking him where he had got his newspaper experience. The stage creaked on; cold seeped into the

13

coach and made Bowman's feet wooden. Mighty unseasonable, this cold; a month ago he'd sweated in his shirt sleeves. He stamped his feet against the floor and, beside him, Pete Beale said, "Damn it! Can't that fellow squeeze any more pull out of those horses?"

Hascomb said soothingly, "We're climbing. It's not a fast road at any season. We should soon reach the change station where we can at least stretch our legs."

Beale suddenly leaned towards the window, his body growing rigid. He brought a Colt's .45 out from under his buffalo coat so fast that Bowman realised the man had been holding the gun ready. The gun's explosion filled the coach, and Beale shouted, "Something moved out there! I saw it!"

The driver's startled cry lifted and came back to them, but the coach rolled on. Bowman, the acrid taste of powder smoke in his mouth, peered out but could see only the moonlit snow and the dark pines beyond the road.

Faro said in an even voice, "Probably a deer. Save your ammunition; we may have need for it, Beale. I shan't fire till I see paint and feathers or hear a warwhoop."

Beale said, "I tell you, I saw something move!" In the semi-darkness, the whites of

14

his eyes showed plain. The stage squealed to a stop, and Beale brought the gun out again. "What's that?"

Bowman looked from his own window. "Driver's picking up my saddle. I told him to watch for it." The saddle thudded above them as the driver heaved it to the railed-in roof. Shortly the coach was moving again.

Hascomb spoke out of the silence that fell among them. "Satterlee ship many cattle this fall, Pete?"

Beale shrugged. "After that winter we had last year? Wasn't enough to bother with. What Kemp's got, he's holding against getting that Broken Wagon beef contract." Suspicion edged his voice. "You just asking? Or are you after something for that paper of yours?"

"Just asking," Hascomb said.

He's trying to put this great lout at his ease, Bowman thought, and he felt a quick admiration for Hascomb and also a sudden irritation that Hascomb should bother. The first reaction had sprung from what Bowman had been; the second came from what he had become. He was forever pulled thus by the old days and the new, he reflected; they made him a mixture of a man. This duality troubled him, for recently he'd fashioned a philosophy that had brought him across the face of Montana and into these hills; and that philosophy must hold, tough and enduring, in the days ahead. But he thought he understood Hascomb's intent. The situation here was a shared thing, and a nervous man was not one they could count on if the attack came. They were four men in a wheeled box, with a fifth above; and they might live through this night together to go their separate ways, or they might die together. Knowing this, Hascomb had tried to pull the grey fear from Beale's mind by speaking of the commonplace.

Faro said, "The question was civil, Beale; the answer fell short of that. Mind your manners when Mr. Hascomb speaks to you."

Beale said, "Damn it, don't rag me!"

Faro shrugged. "You're borrowing trouble before it comes."

And now Bowman had the measure of them all. Fear rode this coach but rested in a different manner on each man's shoulder. Beale was a dullard who answered to instinct like the baited animal he was, Hascomb the wise one who weighed all the factors, Faro the fatalist. And himself? Just as he'd tried his hand at each of their trades, so, too, was he a composite of some part of each of them. He could answer to instinct, but he could also prepare himself for danger, then face that danger as a man faced the turn of a card. But he wished the night and the journey done.

Preposterous, this Sword-Bearer business reaching out to them here! Yet they rode in the shadow of that Crow medicine man with his crazy talk of a magic sword that could annihilate the whites; for his talk had been persuasive enough to bring fifty braves tagging him to the Cheyenne agency, where other bucks had joined up. Some silly matter had started it all — the Piegans raiding the Crows for horses which they drove to the British Possessions and sold — the Crows making reprisals and having their own arrest ordered as a result. And now the Piegans and Crows, whose ancient enmity had stirred up trouble, might be allying against the whites. The Indian agent blamed it all on a visit Sitting Bull had made to the Crows the year before. Who knew where the truth lay? But the Indian scare existed — and fear rode this coach.

Maybe the fear was something deep-rooted in any man old enough to remember wilder years. Maybe, with the first faint drumbeat, time dissolved and the fear branched stark and big. Let's see, Bowman reflected, he'd been twelve just twelve years ago when Yellowstone Valley ranchers, remembering a younger Sitting Bull, had jumped at every sound, and shot at shadows. Like Beale, Bowman could hark up a picture of his father blowing out a lamp and reaching for the rifle racked over the door. He could remember his mother pulling him down into the river-bank brush till an approaching horseman showed close enough to be recognised as a friend.

He shook his head, wanting kinder remembrances; and there were many of them, but he supposed he'd best set his mind against them too. The good memories made the saddlebag on his feet heavy — more of a load than a man could pack. He grew angry with himself; he could not afford softness. Better to think of to-night and what might lie ahead. Suppose all the Indians were indeed harking to Sword-Bearer's distant drum. . . .

Hascomb said, "Moylan took Company A of the Seventh Cavalry from Fort Keogh. An infantry company left with them. He's an old hand, Moylan. He was with Custer, you know." He said this like a man talking to himself, but the words struck so close to Bowman's thinking that he started.

Faro said, "The plan is obviously to overawe Sword-Bearer with a big show of force and so prevent a battle. Maybe it will work."

The driver lifted a shout, and Beale thrust his head from the window and said exultantly, "We're pulling into the change station."

The stage ground to a stop. The driver, swinging down, called, "Twenty minutes while we switch horses. Get yourselves a bite of grub, if you like." Bowman stepped out and saw the tired slump of the driver's shoulders and marked this man's own brand of fear. It was an old man's fear but different from Hascomb's; the driver measured all things by time and distance, and cherished the quick-vanishing years.

Bowman said, "Where is this place?"

"Ten miles below Broken Wagon. Better hump along. We've lost time."

Bowman looked about him. The stage station was a long, low, thatch-roofed building made of rock, and behind it stood a sway-backed barn and an empty corral. Light spilled from the station windows to lie sickly upon the snow. A man came out with a lantern for which there was no real need; the moon stood overhead and laid brightness about. Around him, Bowman saw the snow stretched across an openness pocked by horses' hoofmarks and rutted by the passage of wagons; and beyond, the forest stood, black and forbidding, with the hills rearing to make of this place a bowl cupped deep in rock and trees and winter.

Hascomb alighted and showed himself to be a tall man, slightly stooped of shoulder, his face gentle and tired. Faro wore a black cape and had a long, thin face schooled against being read. Beale was stocky and looked squat and barrel-like in the buffalo coat. He shook himself as a great dog might do and said, "Well, we're this far."

The man with the lantern called, "Any trouble?"

"Nary trouble," the driver said.

And then out yonder the rifle spoke, and the wild whoop lifted.

Beale fell into a crouch, and that ready gun came out and blazed aimlessly; Faro stood frozen, but his still face turned alert. In Bowman there was no real shock. It was as though they had all lived so many hours in the expectation of attack that the attack had been born of their expectation and so was inevitable. He looked toward Hascomb and saw the old man go down to his knees so gently that he might have been kneeling to pray. And then, just as gently, Hascomb fell over.

The rifle had sounded from the trees on the far side of the clearing. It spoke again, and another joined it, and another. Wood splintered from the stage, and the horses began rearing and pitching. Bowman got to Hascomb and hooked his hands under Hascomb's armpits and dragged the man around the stage to the protection of its far side. The banging of guns and the whooping beat steadily at Bowman's ears.

"Get him indoors, someone!" Bowman shouted.

Faro came around the coach and lifted Hascomb. Beale was still exposed; Beale was shooting. Bowman fumbled his sheepskin open and got his gun out. He ran then, coming around the coach and zigzagging across openness, across the snow. He ran diagonally towards the timber and got into it; and only then did he realise he had dropped his saddlebag when he'd leaped to Hascomb's side. He cursed softly and moved through the trees, a stand of snow-mantled fir, and he wondered if he had been wise to manœuvre himself here.

21

The dash to timber had been instinctive. The station walls had offered shelter, but inside a man could be besieged. The openness had held only danger. Here in the woods the fight could be an offence or a defence, as chance dictated.

But suddenly there was no one to fight. He caught a movement in the trees, fired, and felt that he had missed; but as he stood listening, the night turned heavily silent. The shooting had ceased; the whooping had ceased. Distantly, brush crashed to the passage of bodies, and he thought he heard the whinnying of a horse. Sound surged up — the sound of men mounting and riding off, he judged — and then the sound dwindled. Bowman felt himself tremble. He had been drawn tight too long.

Presently he moved on, working towards the spot from which the rifle shots had first come. His worry now was Beale's gun, but that had gone silent, too. He wondered if Beale were down. He came into a clearing large enough for the moonlight to reach into, and here he looked at the trampled snow and even risked a match. He made out moccasin tracks that toed inwards, but there were also the booted tracks of a white man and the stub of a chewed cigar.

Over this sign Bowman pondered, then turned away.

At the edge of the trees he shouted, naming himself, for again he remembered Beale's impetuous gun. Then he walked boldly into the clearing and crossed it towards the station. In the trampled snow near the coach he found his saddlebag where he'd dropped it. He reached and recovered the bag.

CHAPTER TWO

Grey Morning

Pete Beale stood before the stagecoach, his legs planted firmly and his gun in his hand. He looked immovable as an imbedded boulder. He had unbuttoned his buffalo coat to give his arms freer movement, and he was scowling. As Bowman came up, Beale asked, "They're gone?"

Bowman nodded. "They had horses planted back in the timber," he said. "They climbed on to them and lit out. It was a small party. How's Hascomb?"

"He's hurt."

"Hell, I know that," Bowman said impatiently. "How badly?"

"They toted him inside. I ain't had time to find out."

Beale hauled back his buffalo coat and dropped his gun into its holster. No fear showed on that blocky face, and Bowman revised his estimate of the man. There was

24

courage in Beale, the kind of courage that had kept him out here in the open while the attack had lasted. His was a primitive mind that had feared the unknown, his a brute strength that had been impotent against shadows. Once the rifles had sounded, they had brought release to Pete Beale, giving him something tangible to fight. Now he stood chesty and big. "A small party, you said. Crows?"

"I didn't get that close," Bowman said. He shrugged. "We might as well go inside."

The station stood dark now, no lamp-light showing, and when they pushed inside, calling out as they came, Bowman made out a fair-sized room with tables for eating, and a bar running along one wall. At a front window crouched the stage driver, his rifle held ready. Other figures made dim movement in the room.

Bowman called, "You can light up again. I think it's safe."

Someone struck a match and got a lamp burning. He was the man who had come out with the lantern when the stage had rolled up; he was apparently the hostler here, and he had two attendants, and there was a woman, too, a fat Bannack squaw.

To her the hostler said, "Get the other lamps lighted, Maria," and she turned to the task. The hostler motioned his two men towards the door. "Better get those horses changed. One of you can do the chore and the other can stand guard. Get going! If they come back, they can't cross the clearing without your seeing them."

"But they can pick us off from the edge of the woods," one of the men said.

Bowman shook his head. "They won't bother. They could have done that any time. They waited out there awhile. It was the stage they were waiting for."

Beale asked sharply, "How's that?"

"I read the sign," Bowman said. "They waited, I tell you. If it was the station they figured on wiping out, why did they hang around until there were five more guns to buck?"

Beale had propped himself against the bar. He shoved back his broad-brimmed hat and scratched his tousled head. "Now what do you make of that?"

Bowman said, "I'm new to these parts. All I know about this Broken Wagon section is that it started booming a few months ago. Gold strike, wasn't it? Tell me, has there been any outlawry?"

"A few hold-ups. One drunken miner rolling another for his dust. Nothing big and organised like they had at Bannack or

Virginia City in the sixties."

The hostler said, "There ain't been a hold-up fat enough to make headlines since Bart Carney's day. You've heard of Carney, I reckon. It ain't over ten, fifteen miles from here that he stopped the Billings-Helena stage and lifted twenty thousand dollars. He got twenty years in Deer Lodge pen for that little frolic."

Beale showed a scowling, troubled face in the lamplight. "Are you trying to make out this was a hold-up instead of an Indian attack? None of us is gold-fat miners. We're just some people who had business of one kind and another in Helena. I happened to be doing some chores for Kemp Satterlee, my boss. Who's packing anything worth stealing?" His glance dropped to the saddlebag Bowman carried. "You, maybe?"

"They weren't looking for me," Bowman said flatly. "They were Indians, all right. I saw the tracks. But this still doesn't add up to an Indian attack. In the old days, where was the first place the Indians struck when they decided to go on the warpath? A stage station. That way they got horses. But this outfit waited." He wondered if he should tell them the rest of it — that a white man had waited out there, too. Or had it been a breed, answering to his wilder blood? He didn't know, and he had a graver concern. He looked about. "Where's Hascomb?"

The hostler shook his head. "He's bad hurt. I had him put in my own bed. That gambler's in there with him." He indicated a door leading to a side room.

"I'll go see him," Bowman said.

He picked up one of the lamps the squaw had lighted, went over, and pushed open the door. Hascomb lay stretched upon a high-backed bed, and Faro stood bending over him. Working by whatever moonlight had fallen through the one window of the room, the gambler had got the man's coats off, opened Hascomb's shirt front, and got a crude pad tied over a wound in his chest. Bowman placed the lamp upon a small table near the bed so that the light fell upon Hascomb without blinding him. Hascomb's breathing was a harsh rasp. Bowman looked at him and knew that he was dying.

Faro knew it, too. The knowledge was bitter on his face as he straightened up. He had removed his hat, and Bowman saw that his hair, long and thick and curling, was shot with grey and that he was much older than he'd looked in the moonlight.

Bowman said, "The attacking party took off."

Faro said with quiet desperation, "Miles needs a doctor. There's none nearer than Broken Wagon. Are those horses changed yet?"

Bowman said, "Hell, you can't get to the camp and back with a doctor. Not in time."

Anger stirred Faro. "Do you have to be so damn' brutal?"

Bowman shrugged. "If Hascomb runs a newspaper, he deals in facts."

"He's right," Hascomb said. His voice was surprisingly firm and held no rancour. "The bullet is in too dangerous a place to go after it with a knife." His face was gaunt against the pillow, and he was, Bowman decided, the bravest man beneath this roof at this moment. There was kindliness in him, and wisdom, and no compromise with truth. It was this last that hit Bowman, knowing how few men attained the honesty to look at themselves and see a clear image.

Bowman said, "You're not dead yet. We'll do everything we can for you."

Hascomb said, "Then tell me this, Neil Bowman. Would you like to buy a half interest in the Broken Wagon *Bugle*?"

Bowman stared at him. This seemed a wild question at such a time, as though fever had got hold of Hascomb and made him queer-minded. Bowman shook his head. "I wasn't intending to stop at Broken Wagon. I caught the stage only because I had no horse. I hope to get one at the camp."

Hascomb said intently, "This is not a chance I'd offer any man. The *Bugle* is a going concern; it belongs to me and my daughter. With it goes a fight, and that's why I want it in the right hands. I'll make you a good price — five thousand dollars for a half interest. Faro will tell you my assets are worth nearly three times that much."

"Some tramp journalist will come along," Bowman said. "Boom camps draw them. There'll be a man to step in."

"I want to have seen that man," Hascomb said.

"Why me?"

"You are a brave man; you showed that when the rifles started banging. You're considerate, too; you dragged me to safety when you might have been running for cover. And you can think: you carried the fight to the timber. Faro told me so. You'll find my daughter at Broken Wagon,

Bowman." He began to cough; he rallied and made his voice firm again. "There's a man who won't let her keep the *Bugle* unless she runs it on his terms. She has only old Ben Hare, my printer, to stand by her, and he's a frail reed for anyone to lean on. I've got to have a man like you. I've got to!"

Bowman scowled. "If you have a printer and a press, any friend of yours should be able to do the rest. What about you, Faro?"

"No," Faro said. "You see, I work for the opposition."

Bowman started, remembering the obvious signs of friendship between these two and seeing Faro here, at the bedside, with his grief so plain on him.

Faro spread his hands. "My only skill is at cards. I play those cards as a houseman for Sig Ogden. Have you ever heard of him?"

"Never," Bowman said.

"Every boom camp attracts at least one like him," Faro said. "We have a miners' council, but he twists it to his own fancy. We have a judge, but he owns the judge. Whatever Broken Wagon becomes will be of Ogden's making, unless someone opposes him. Miles was doing that."

"Ogden," Bowman said softly. "He's a new one to me." And though this was true,

31

his mind was swept again to those old days in the Yellowstone Valley and the life he'd put forever behind him. An Ogden had been there, too, but with a different name, a different face. The world was full of Ogdens, no matter what they called themselves. They dragged long spurs across the grass; they threw wide shadows upon the hills. Thinking this, an old urge grew in him, knuckle-tightening and heady. But he remembered the new philosophy he'd held to in the stagecoach as it threaded the snowy miles, the philosophy that had brought him into these hills and would take him towards far, new horizons. He had no business in Broken Wagon. He felt caught up in indecision, pulled this way and that.

He'd been about to shake his head, but instead he said, "You spoke of a half interest. No, I'd have to be the boss. No girl could stand in the way of whatever I chose to do."

Hascomb said quickly, "Agreed. Faro, there's a notebook and pencil in my inner coat pocket. Get it and write what I tell you."

Beale thrust his head into the room. "The horses are changed. We've been waiting. How many of you are coming?"

Bowman waved him away. "Go buy yourself a drink. We're not moving yet."

Beale frowned. "Hurry it up, damn it." But he withdrew from the doorway.

"That notebook, Faro," Hascomb said urgently.

Faro got the notebook and pencil with evident reluctance. "Miles, I'm not sure you're being wise."

Feebly Hascomb lifted his hand. Was it sheer nerve that sustained him, Bowman wondered. Hascomb said, "Maybe I can read men, too, Faro. And maybe I'm the gambler now. I can only play the hand that has been dealt me to-night. Surely you understand? Will you write, my friend?"

Faro opened the notebook.

"For one dollar and other valuable considerations, I hereby sell, convey, and assign to Neil Bowman a half interest in my property called the Broken Wagon *Bugle*," Hascomb dictated. "Said half interest to apply to all equipment, supplies, furnishings, and goodwill. Be it understood that the said Neil Bowman is to occupy a managerial position on the newspaper and have full rein to dictate its policies and to conduct the publishing in any manner of his choosing. . . . I think that should do it."

Faro shook his head. "What's to keep him from selling the paper to-morrow? To Ogden, for instance."

Hascomb thought about this. He looked greyer in the lamplight; he looked spent and old. "Add these words, Faro: it is further understood that at no time within a period of five years shall Neil Bowman transfer the ownership or —"

"No!" Bowman interjected. "I'll not have my hands tied that way. Word it something like this: It is further understood that at no time shall Neil Bowman dispose of the property where such disposal may be construed to be against the best interests of his partner, Miss — What do you call her?"

"Jenny," Hascomb said. "Write it as he worded it, Faro."

Faro shook his head. "And trust to his conscience?"

"That's the hand that's been dealt."

Faro shrugged. A strong man, or a weak one, Bowman wondered. Strong enough to stand up for Hascomb's rights, obviously, yet unwilling to make a fighting issue of them. Perhaps it was the man's inherent fatalism that made him like that.

Faro finished his scribbling and passed the notebook to Bowman. Bowman read it

34

carefully, and nodded. Faro took the note book and held it so that Hascomb could scrawl his signature. Faro added his own signature as witness.

"Give it to him," Hascomb directed.

"We haven't seen the colour of his money," Faro said bluntly.

"He wouldn't be carrying it with him. Again we have to go on trust, Faro."

"There's no guarantee that he owns more than his saddle and the bag he's carrying," Faro said stubbornly. "You're thinking only of Sig Ogden, Miles. I'm remembering Jenny."

"I'm remembering Jenny, too," Hascomb said. "It's the man I want, not the money. Don't you see? If he has only the dollar the agreement mentions, it will still be the best deal I can make to-night."

Bowman said in a hard, flat voice, "The money is here," and he tossed the saddlebag at Faro.

Faro caught it, opened it, and peered inside. His face showed full surprise. "Currency!" he said. "It's stuffed with currency!"

Bowman reached across the bed and retrieved the bag. He was already sorry that he'd let himself be goaded into showing the money. "If you like, you can be present when I count out five thousand to Jenny Hascomb."

Beale thrust his head through the doorway again. "You coming?"

Bowman said, "We're staying here. Maybe for an hour — maybe for the rest of the night. If the driver wants to go on, he can. Go tell him what I said."

Beale disappeared and Bowman looked across the bed at Faro. Wordlessly, they both found chairs and seated themselves. Hascomb closed his eyes, and his breathing became harsher. Bowman got sleepy. He had the sensation of being in a trance; there was no reality to the things that had happened to-night. A senseless Indian attack. A dying man making a desperate bargain. And now a newspaper in his control; but when he turned this over in his mind, he couldn't remember how he'd been persuaded or why he'd let himself be.

After a while Faro said in a strained voice, "I still think I should get a horse and make a fast run for the camp."

Bowman shook his head. "There never was a chance. Hascomb knew that all along."

The driver peered through the doorway, looking at Hascomb. "How is he?"

"Sleeping," Bowman said. "You're not going on?"

"After a while," the driver said. His old face turned bland. "No point in riskin' another Indian attack. I've pointed that out to Pete Beale. He's decided to drink hisself stupid at the bar." His glance moved back to Hascomb, and his eyes softened. "A good man," he said.

"Yes," said Faro. "A good man."

"I think he's gone," Bowman said.

But Hascomb was still breathing; he was to lie like this for an hour, and another, somewhere in a shadowy realm that was neither sleep nor death. The lamp burned itself out, and grey morning crowded against the window and gave harsh outline to everything in the room. Bowman looked at Faro and wondered if he himself showed so haggard a face.

Faro stirred and said, "Maybe we should go on. There is nothing more we can do for him."

Hascomb's eyes came open, and he stared about, trying to focus on Bowman. He had a wild, startled look, and his voice was so weak that both men had to bend close to hear him. Hascomb said, "I remember where I heard your name —"

Bowman said, "It needn't matter. Do

37

you hear me? It needn't matter."

He wasn't sure whether his words reached through to Hascomb, who'd closed his eyes again. But Hascomb smiled slightly, and smiling, died. It was a full minute before either man realised this, and then Faro gently pulled the blanket over Hascomb's face.

He looked across at Bowman and asked, "What did he mean, there at the end?"

"It's no business of yours," Bowman said.

He stood up, feeling stiff and wooden. He picked the saddlebag from the floor and walked out into the main room, and Faro came after him. The hostler and his Indian wife were not in sight; probably they had bedded in the barn. The driver sat dozing in a chair at one of the tables; Beale had his head on his folded arms at another table, a battle before him.

Bowman roused the driver. "Come on," Bowman said. "We're heading for Broken Wagon."

The driver looked towards the bedroom. "He's gone?"

Bowman nodded.

"Will you be taking his body along?" the driver asked.

Faro spoke up. "I'll send a wagon

down," he said stiffly. "He's not to be toted like a piece of baggage."

"I'll git the horses hitched up," the driver said. "I had them put back in the barn." He lumbered outside, and Bowman walked towards the door with Faro only half a step behind him. Faro touched his shoulder.

"Yes, Miles is gone," Faro said. "But I remain. Just remember that. Miles made the best bargain he could, but I'm not sure it was a good bargain. Do you understand?"

"Yes," Bowman said. "I understand. And there's somethng else I'll keep in mind. You belong to the opposition. You said so yourself, remember."

CHAPTER THREE

Clash and Challenge

They rolled into Broken Wagon in mid-morning, and Bowman stepped down from the coach into the turmoil of the boom camp and shook his head, thinking that here was another thing as misplaced in time as Sword-Bearer's attempted uprising. Broken Wagon should have belonged to the 1860's, when Bannack and Virginia City and Last Chance Gulch had wildly flourished; here was another such collection of log and canvas and hasty shacks as had marked the beginnings of the earlier camps. Broken Wagon sprawled along the sunless bottom of a gulch and up the slopes; buildings perched everywhere. No pattern here. No purpose but the moment's purpose. No beauty. The main street lay at the lowest level and followed the serpentine windings of the gulch. Planks served for walks, and upon them booted men moved restlessly.

Freight wagons creaked along the frozen ruts, and from somewhere the music of a hurdy-gurdy house spilled out upon the day.

Bowman got his saddle from the driver, but he dropped it in a corner of the stage station; and carrying only the saddlebag, he breasted his way along the clogged street. No placering now, with the ice choking the streams; miners from the fingering gulches and the high, shouldering hills burned out their restiveness in all the saloons. Still, he was surprised to find so many men in the camp, until he remembered the Indian scare and realised it had driven men from lonely claims to the protection of the camp. Bowman was astonished to see Indians here, too; a stolid, blanketed row of them squatted before one of the saloons. Wanderers from a nearby reservation, he supposed.

He was looking for quarters. Faro had told him there was a hotel, but he walked past it, not liking the close and crowded look of the two-story structure, so new that the lumber was still green. Men jostled each other under the wooden overhang of the porch, and tramped in and out of the hotel door making a great clamour in the lobby. Four thousand men here, Faro had said on the way up from the change station in the frigid dawn.

On that ride, Bowman had wanted to talk about Sig Ogden and the fight Miles Hascomb had been having with Ogden, but Faro had turned that subject aside. Bowman got an inkling of the reason for the gambler's reluctance; it was Pete Beale's burly presence. But Faro had been willing enough to talk about the camp. He'd been hard hit by Miles Hascomb's death, and perhaps for him talking had been a medicine. Certainly that moment of clash between him and Bowman just as they'd left the change station had not made Faro withdrawn.

"Broken Wagon?" Faro had said as they rolled along. "An inelegant name, but fitting. Came about because of old Sam Marble. He's one of that breed of prospectors who always came too late for the other man's big strike, but kept looking. Twenty-five years he kept looking. People he met in bars in Helena and Butte and Bozeman staked him. He led a packhorse ten thousand miles through all the mountains. Then he acquired a wagon. An old, patched-together buckboard that someone gave him, probably. With that he could haul supplies as far as the roads went and then

42

carry the stuff in. Last spring he was taking this road we're on now. It leads up through the gulch and over the hump to the cattle country where Beale, here, works. A lot of men had prospected this vicinity in the old days and found colour, but not enough. Marble's wagon broke down this side of the hump. Just fell apart, they say. Nothing for him to do but camp till he could get his wagon fixed. He started panning nearby, and he struck it rich. He staked out the discovery claim, and the news spread. Now we've got a town called Broken Wagon, and nearly half a million in gold has come out of it."

Bowman had nodded. Here was another legend akin to Bill Fairweather's panning for tobacco money and making the fabulous Alder Gulch strike. Or the four Georgians' taking a last chance at the gulch that came to bear that name and be the birthplace of Helena. Between thirty and forty million dollars had come out of Alder Gulch the first five years of operations; and even as recently as a couple of years ago, the annual take had been better than a quarter of a million. Last Chance Gulch had been sweet, too.

And now there was Broken Wagon. Bowman had known more about the development here than he'd let on, but he hadn't heard the story of how the camp had come by its name. A good story, he decided. Well, every man rolled along in his wagon, and sometimes the wagon broke down. It happened to him, and so there were years he wanted to forget. But then, too, there was that saddlebag. . . .

Walking this Whitewater Gulch where Broken Wagon sprawled, he hefted the saddlebag and remembered the five thousand dollars of its contents that was pledged to a purchase. He wondered if Faro was at this moment telling Jenny Hascomb what had happened last night. There'd been no girl that Bowman had seen waiting at the stage station.

He was tired. The weight of last night was on him and the sour feeling that he'd been caught up in a rush of events and plunged towards a future not of his choosing. Somehow Hascomb, dying, had managed to outfox him, manœuvring their deal so that he, Bowman, had found himself committed. When he tried again going over their talk in his mind, it was still fuzzy and unreal. He knew that he needed to sleep.

He might have gone back to the hotel. Instead, he turned off the main street —

Placer, he noticed it was called; there was a signpost at a corner — and began ascending the north slope of the gulch. Halfway up he reached a house set on the slope in such a manner that its two stories were both at ground level, and he saw that this house bore a sign: ROOM FOR RENT. He'd climbed with the notion of having a look at Broken Wagon from the vantage the slope would give him, but now he turned in at the house and knocked on the door. The place was built of logs, and the chinking looked tighter than most he'd seen here. From where he stood beneath the broad eaves, he could look over his shoulder to the far slope and beyond it to the high lift of snow-burdened peaks. Below, Placer Street sprawled, a collection of buildings strewn haphazardly as by a giant hand.

He knocked again and the door opened, and a woman said, "Yes — ?"

Whatever he'd been prepared for in the way of a landlady, it was no such woman as this. She was perhaps thirty, but her eyes were older and showed a thousand years' experience. Her face was oval, handsome, and reserved, yet a certain sadness stood plain. Her hair was brass yellow and piled high, and her body was full and rounded beneath a dress that had become too tight. He had seen a few women on the planking below; they were bonneted housewives and girls from the hurdy-gurdies and the saloons. This woman belonged to neither.

"I'd like to see the room you have," he said.

She inclined her head. "Come in."

He moved past her and stood in a parlour with an organ and a sewing table and some tastefully arranged horsehair furniture. The rug was worn, but it had been a good one. On a wall a framed crayon portrait, probably copied and enlarged from a tintype, dominated the room by virtue of the leashed fury in the face it portrayed. A bearded face with burning, compelling eyes. Her father, he wondered? The picture held him in spite of himself, and he stood staring until he heard her say, "My work. A copying job, of course. My speciality was still life — flowers and vases and such. It's a childish pastime I've outgrown."

She beckoned and led him beyond this room into a kitchen and up a short flight of stairs. Her movement was sinuous enough to stir him. She opened the door of a small bedroom, plain but comfortable. She said, "This will be fifty dollars a week." The price surprised him until he remembered that this was a boom camp with boom prices.

"I'll take it," he said. "My name is Neil Bowman."

"I am Mrs. Addison," she said. "Helen Addison."

"You have other roomers."

"None," she said, and her lips turned firm, closing out any other question he might have asked.

"I'll want to shave," he said.

"Call me and I'll fetch you hot water."

She turned and left him. He shoved the saddlebag under the bed and sat down upon the edge of the bed, and tiredness smote him like an axe. He tugged off his boots and shrugged out of the sheepskin and let it fall on the floor. He managed to get his gun belt off, too. He was trying to pull up the blankets as sleep caught him. . . .

When he awoke, he judged that it was mid-afternoon. He sat up and had that moment of strangeness that comes from awakening in new surroundings. He opened the door and called to Mrs. Addison, and she fetched him a pitcher of hot water and departed, saying nothing. He shaved, then opened the saddlebag and counted out five thousand dollars and thrust that great bundle of currency inside his shirt front. Again he shoved the saddlebag under the bed. There was a key in the door, he discovered. He locked the door and came down through the house. He did not see Mrs. Addison. In the parlour, the crayon portrait scowled at him, and he had the strange sensation that the eyes followed him across the room. He found his way to the front door and let himself out.

The sky stood leaden above Broken Wagon, but the air did not seem to be nearly so cold. He trudged down the slant and found a restaurant on Placer. The place was made of planking roofed over by canvas, and it was crowded and noisy. And draughty. Winter seeped through the walls, and men brought the winter in with them, clinging to their clothes. He had no kinship with these men, and in the idle moments as he ate, he saw them as ants scurrying over the hills and into the canyons, each with a dream of riches to come, each following his own slovenly destiny to some slovenly end. Give them the gold of their seeking and what would be changed? He felt like a stranger to them; he had become a stranger to all humanity, and he had no patience with people who stirred themselves busily to no solid purpose.

He thought, A horse beneath me and I could be gone. The idea mounted to a strong temptation.

His meal finished, he came out upon Placer again and began looking around for the Broken Wagon *Bugle*, stirred more by curiosity than any real interest. The way this street straggled, there was no point from which he could get a full look at it. Yonder, a bell tower lifted against the sky; fire was a constant hazard in the mining camps, and he understood the fear that had put the big brass bell up there. He began moving along and so came abreast of the largest of the saloons. The sign said, THE IMPERIAL — SIGMUND OGDEN, PROP.

He turned inside and saw the place through a haze. Miners had dragged the mud of the street in upon the planking, where, drying, it had been stirred to dust by other boots until it now rose and filled the air. Men crammed the place, and the smell of wool and sweat was here. Men clustered around the gaming tables and stood elbow to elbow at the bar. Bowman wedged a place for himself and called for whisky. When it was served, he slapped a gold piece on the bar.

Behind him, a man said, "No, my friend. The first one is on the house."

Bowman had only to raise his eyes to the bar mirror. This man was tall and stooped and wore a shawl draped over his shoulders, partly covering a suit coat of fine black material and excellent cut. His face was bony, the forehead high, and the eyes deep set. A good wind might have blown him away but for some solid strength that lay deep and was revealed in those eyes. Bowman made his quick guess and said, "You'd be Sig Ogden."

"And you would be Neil Bowman."

Bowman said, "Then Faro has already reported to you."

"I've not seen him," Ogden said, his lips showing faint amusement. "He does not come to work till evening. At present he's probably consoling the bereaved daughter of a dear friend."

"Beale, then?" Bowman guessed.

Ogden shrugged. "It doesn't matter. I concede that Beale spoke of you. A mouthy man, Pete. He regaled this establishment earlier to-day with an account of how he stood off a horde of bloodthirsty savages at the change station last night. I gathered there were at least a thousand Indians. I was much more interested in a few words he'd overheard and a few things he'd surmised. Tell me, is it true that you are now the owner of the *Bugle*?"

"Half owner."

"It's a property that interests me," Ogden said. "Shall we go to my office and talk about it?" He nodded towards a flight of stairs leading to the upper story.

"I think not," Bowman said. He filled his glass from the bottle that had been put before him, lifted the drink, and downed it.

Ogden still showed only that faint amusement. "Beale didn't overhear enough to learn the price. It doesn't matter. Whatever it was, I'll double it. How is that for a fat profit and a quick turnover?"

"Not interested," Bowman said. "Not to-day, anyway."

"And why not?" Ogden asked.

Why not? A man might make a bargain and regret it and wonder afterwards how the bargain had come to be. A man might think of a horse to be bought and the trail that led out of here. But now the question had been put to him, and an answer had to be made. He might have said that his bargain with Hascomb had held a joker that kept him from selling, but he'd made

51

Hascomb toss the joker out of the deck. Now he knew why he had done so, just as he knew in this instant exactly why he'd let himself be persuaded to Miles Hascomb's proposition. He turned around and put his back to the bar and propped his elbows on it and faced Ogden.

"Why not?" he said. "Because I don't like you."

"That's ridiculous," Ogden said. "You've never seen me before." He kept his voice low; they might have been two men discussing the weather. Around them others moved and jostled and made their loud talk, but these two were an island in the boisterousness.

"Ah, but I *have* seen you," Bowman said. He fingered his empty glass; the whisky lay warm in his stomach, and exhilaration coursed through him. "I've seen you many times. Sometimes you're tall and sometimes you're short. Sometimes you're bright and sometimes just muscle-heavy. The way I remember you most clearly is with wide shoulders and curly red whiskers and a pair of legs sprung by too much riding. You came into the Yellowstone Valley with Texas cattle, and you sweated, froze, and starved like everyone else, but you prospered faster because there was nothing you wouldn't turn your hand to. Do you follow me?"

Ogden had grown cold and remote. "Perhaps I do," he said. "Go on."

"In twenty years you'd made yourself a cattle king, big enough to buy judges and juries. There was one two-bit rancher, though, who didn't like the notion of being shoved off the land where his mother and father were buried. He bucked you, so one fine day the sheriff rode out and found a hide in his barn with your brand burned into it. After that, there was a farce of a trial. The jury walked in with one shoulder lower than the other from the gold they packed in their pockets, and the judge couldn't quite meet the two-bit rancher's eye. But you sat to the front of the courtroom smiling and combing your whiskers with your fingers and looking like a wolf at the kill."

Ogden shook his head. "And so some friend of yours got framed into prison, and you've hated all the big men of the world ever since."

"Not the big men. The small, scheming ones who think that the jangle of gold will buy them anything."

Ogden said evenly, "Then you're a fool."

"No," Bowman said. "I *was* a fool. That

day is over. There may come a time when I'll drive a bargain with you, but it will be on my terms. Meanwhile I'll take pleasure in giving you a tougher fight than even Miles Hascomb would have given you. Do we understand each other?"

"Perfectly," Ogden said. His eyes had turned muddy, but his lips were smiling again.

"Then I'll buy my own drink," Bowman said, and he left the coin lying on the bar as he brushed past Ogden and shouldered his way towards the door.

CHAPTER FOUR

The Schemers

From the steps of the Imperial, Bowman recognised the *Bugle* office by the plate glass window bearing the newspaper's name. The building stood diagonally across from Ogden's saloon. Crossing over, Bowman saw something else, a flat-bed wagon with a tired-looking team hitched to it and upon the wagon a plain pine box. Thus had Miles Hascomb been fetched home. That sight stopped Bowman. There was a finality in the harsh outline of the box that made the presence of death more real than had the sight of an empty husk stretched upon a bed in the change station. There Hascomb had looked like a tired man at last finding rest. Unseen in a coffin, he was irrevocably dead, his dream spun out. That was the difference, and its impact on Bowman was harder than he'd supposed it would be.

Men had gathered about the wagon and

were making talk with Hascomb's name threaded through it. Bowman moved on, walking in the shadow of his own sombre thoughts.

A man plucked at his sleeve and asked, "You wouldn't have the price of a meal, partner?" Bowman stepped back from the strong reek of whisky on the fellow. A tall man, this one, tall as Bowman and of about the same build, a man who shivered in his shirt sleeves and needed a shave. Wherever the flame of easy riches burned brightest, there were these hapless ones.

Bowman shrugged. "Do you mean the price of a meal or the price of a drink?"

The man said, "Maybe it's a blanket I'd buy. There's an empty shack high on the north slope where I've been bunking, but it's mighty cold these nights. I'm done with drinking, partner. I swear it."

Bowman took off his sheepskin. "Take this," he said. He didn't care much for that sheepskin; it was a garment of expediency he'd been given at a back-country ranch when the cold weather had struck. "I'll make a bet that you'll turn it in for a bottle inside an hour."

"You'll lose that bet," the man said as he hauled on the sheepskin.

Bowman watched him go and wondered

56

at his own impulse. There was some kind of softness in him, he supposed, some holdover from what he'd once been. Just an hour ago he'd told himself he was a stranger to all humanity. Half angry, he turned in at the *Bugle*'s office.

Jenny Hascomb sat in a swivel chair before a roll-top desk, but she had turned the chair around so that her back was to the desk. She sat with her hands folded in her lap, and his first impression was of her eyes; they were big and sombre, and vacant with grief, but she had not been crying. She was alone. He wondered if Faro had just left and almost wished that Faro was here. He felt embarrassed. He said, "I'm Neil Bowman."

She looked straight through him. "Yes," she said. "And I'm Jenny Hascomb."

She was, he judged, a tall girl. She was black haired, fair skinned, and slender. She troubled him. He couldn't have put a name to what he'd expected of her at their first meeting, but it had not been indifference. She was no more than nineteen, yet he had the feeling that she was old in the same way as Mrs. Addison, and maybe wiser. An urge to break through her indifference made him reach inside his shirt for the currency he'd stowed there. He walked

57

over and dumped the money on the desk.

"Faro told you about the deal?" he asked.

"Yes. Aren't you first going to look at what you're buying?"

"I've already looked," he said with irony, and he was thinking of Sig Ogden. But he let his gaze rove about. This office was a small space dominated by the desk and a pot-bellied stove that glowed red to-day. There was also a littered pine table; heaps of proofs lay piled upon it and some wrapped jobs of printing. The place had a smell of paper and glue and ink. A door led to the rear of the building, and he stepped to this door and saw a Campbell power press and type founts and compositors' slate-topped tables. The new Mergenthaler typesetting machine hadn't penetrated to Broken Wagon; as he'd expected, this shop still did its setting by hand. No one was at work in the rear room, and he remembered Hascomb's reference to the printer, Ben Hare. He again faced the girl.

"Faro also told you the terms of the deal?"

"Yes," she said. "Ben sets type, runs the press, and does whatever else strikes his fancy. Miles often let him go through the mail and telegraph stuff and boil it down to what we needed. I address wrappers and bring in advertising and read proof. The rest of the work was Miles's. Now it will be yours."

"When should the next issue go out?"

"Four days from now."

"That will give me time to get the feel of the camp. Then I'll decide our policy." He watched her closely as he said this; he thought her lips tightened slightly. He added, "Am I going to have opposition from you?"

"Sooner or later, probably," she said. "I see you carry a chip on your shoulder. I'm not sure of you yet. A few minutes ago I looked from the window and saw you give your coat to a down-and-outer."

"I could have given him money, but I didn't. What I gave him was warmth. If he prefers to trade it for whisky, the choice — and the fault — will be his."

"So your generosity has a hard core to it," she said bitterly. "Generosity shouldn't hold protection for the giver. There's a side to you I'm not going to like."

He shrugged. "This is no time for us to be circling each other like cat and dog." And then, because the question had to be asked: "When will you hold the funeral?"

"Late this afternoon."

"So soon?"

She nodded. "Just as quickly as they can get a grave dug in frozen earth. What point would there be in delaying? Miles would want it over and done."

"Have you always called your father Miles?"

"We thought of ourselves as partners first — father and daughter second. You think that's harsh? We never could afford sentimentality, he and I. I remember other camps like this, and cow towns, too. Sometimes he worked on another man's paper; sometimes he had his own. His pen had a sting to it, and more than once we had to move along in the dark of the moon. All I remember is running. He was kindly, but he never learned what I had to learn before I was ten. My philosophy is quite simple. I try to hit first before somebody hits me, but I don't go looking for quarrels. Does that help you to understand?"

He shook his head. Pure rock, he thought, harder than anything in these hills. Her loveliness was a lie then, and he supposed her smile would be as bitter as the hundred cold campfires she and Miles Hascomb had put behind them. She stood up now and proved to be as tall as he'd thought. She was well rounded, utterly feminine to the eye, but with no more warmth than the Campbell press back there in the other room.

"Is there anything else?" she asked.

He took this as a dismissal and turned towards the door. "No," he said. Then he paused. "Try to cry," he urged. "Let it all come out of you."

She stared at him. "I never learned to cry. There wasn't time. Anyway, the big things were always too big to cry over, and the small things were too petty."

"Good day," he said and stepped out into the street. The wind struck him sharply. He would have to go and buy himself a coat.

Looking across his office at Kemp Satterlee, Sig Ogden found little to his liking about the rancher. Satterlee didn't belong here, he realised. In these quarters over the Imperial, Ogden lived and conducted his spider-web business, and he had made the place a flattering reflection of some facets of his personality. The rugs, from Helena, were soft to the foot. The furniture was an accumulation of the years; each piece spoke its own story to Ogden and brought him a remembrance from some closed chapter in his life. Yonder oak sideboard, intricately scrolled, had come from Virginia City; the chair in which Satterlee sprawled had known Butte. But Satterlee made a wrong note in the room, throwing all of it out of tune.

Satterlee was, Ogden thought, more ox than man. Wide shouldered, thick necked, and big handed, the rancher might have been older brother to his own foreman, Pete Beale. The difference was that Satterlee was far craftier and therefore more dangerous. The animal power of the man offended Ogden. Whether men were for or against him, he preferred them to be rapiers, rather than clubs. Moreover, Satterlee in building by brute power had grown careless in crafty games, even though he had a talent for craftiness. This knowledge gave Ogden a further sense of unease to-day and made his voice petulant.

"I've told you time and again always to come up the back way," he said. "Who knows who might have been in the bar and seen you head up here? Do you want our partnership shouted from the roofs?"

Satterlee was drinking whisky — Ogden's whisky. His huge legs thrust before him, he held up the glass to the light and looked at it, smug and comfortable.

"Nobody down there who would have made any difference. Oh, maybe Ben Hare. But he wasn't paying me any heed."

Ogden said irritably, "Nobody knows who Ben Hare might have been looking at or what he might have been thinking."

Satterlee grinned. "You're too nervous, Sig. You'll worry yourself into an early grave. Hell, isn't this a day for celebration?"

"Another thing," Ogden said. "You've got those Indians of yours in town. Is that wise?"

"Maybe. Lots of talk to-day about the ruckus at the change station. Lots of jumpiness about Indians. Suppose folks got to wondering about which Indians were where. My boys are sitting in plain sight. It might kind of take the edge off suspicion. A man starts sneaking, he invites talk. Maybe it's likewise better that I *did* use the front stairs."

Ogden said, "If the Miners' Council gives me a contract to supply the winter's beef for this camp, they still mustn't wake up to the fact that you'll be supplying the beef. One whisper could ruin us. You know that, Kemp."

"And who's to start the whispering? Not Miles Hascomb with his damn' paper."

"There's Bowman now. I've told you about him, and you saw me talking to him."

"Just a drifter in a sheepskin coat with one button missing, Sig. I'll find a way to take care of him."

"But meantime you've got to be careful. Suppose Ben Hare did pick up an item this afternoon. Suppose it reads, 'Kemp Satterlee paid a call on Sig Ogden at the Imperial last week. Does Ogden plan on getting beef from Satterlee to supply this camp?' Some little thing like that, and you've got the miners talking."

"Likely Ben will be drifting now that Hascomb's dead. Maybe this Bowman won't even want him around the premises. Ben's only half a bargain at best."

"I wonder," Ogden said. He turned thoughtful. "You've given me an idea," he said finally. He crossed to the door, opened it, and shouted down into the barroom from the head of the stairs. He stood waiting, and shortly one of his bartenders came puffing to the upper landing.

"Is Ben Hare still boozing down there?" Ogden asked.

The bartender nodded.

"Tell him I'd like to see him," Ogden said. He turned to Satterlee. "Step into the

64

bedroom while he's here."

"Sure," Satterlee said. He hauled himself out of the chair and parted the curtains at the doorway of Ogden's sleeping quarters. Ogden heard footsteps on the stairs. The bartender came hesitantly to the landing; he frowned.

"Ben's gone?" Ogden asked.

"No, he's still below. He wants to know did you say please."

Ogden scowled. "What sort of drunken nonsense is that?"

"I don't know. But I don't think he'll come unless you say please."

Ogden's chagrin changed to amusement. "Tell him please ten times over. Just see that he gets started up here."

"Okay," the bartender said.

From the bedroom, Satterlee guffawed heartily. "My god, Sig, how independent can a man get?"

"Never mind," Ogden said. "That free spirit of his can work for us just as well as against us. Hush, now. He's coming."

Leaving the door open, Ogden moved back to the captain's chair before his ornate desk. He was seated when Ben Hare framed himself in the doorway, seeming to teeter there, a tall, lank man with tousled mouse-coloured hair and a wrinkled face that might have been kindly save for the perpetual wickedness of the eyes. Hare was, Ogden judged, somewhere near seventy. The man was wearing a rusty black suit to-day and a string tie.

Ogden said, "Come in, Ben."

Ben Hare made a low bow. "My congratulations to you," he said. "And may you burn brightly in hell."

"For what?" Ogden asked.

"Same reason for both. We bury Miles this afternoon."

"I might be just as sorry as you. I liked Miles."

"So," Hare said and squinted his eyes nearly closed and twisted up the corners of his mouth. He looked ready either to laugh or cry. "If you've sent for me so we can hold a wake together, you'll have to supply the whisky."

"Help yourself," Ogden said and waved towards the sideboard. As Hare crossed towards it, he added, "As a matter of fact, I sent for you to offer you a job."

"So — ? Going to print your own labels for your whisky bottles?"

Ogden said, "I have many ventures. The Imperial is one. My claim is another. You know that I may be building a packing plant. I might like to start a newspaper, too."

"And what would you pay for the services of a first-class magician?"

"Magician?"

"Surely," said Hare. He poured himself a generous drink and took a generous swig from it. "The homeliest mud-fence of a girl can take unto herself a husband; but when I set up the incident in type, she becomes a beautiful and charming bride and it is intimated that a thousand cast-aside suitors are drowning themselves in their own tears. Or take the dullest bore who ever moved the buttons on his waistcoat to accommodate his growing paunch: put him on a stump to twist the eagle's tail, and I convert him into a spellbinding orator who held an audience enthralled. Am I not a magician?" He smacked his lips. "And by the way, this is far better whisky than you serve at your bar."

"That's truth, not magic," Ogden said. "So is this: I'll pay twice as much as Miles paid you, with the understanding that you start to work for me right now."

Hare puckered up his face. "Hasty bargains are often regretted, if I may coin an old saying. I must sleep on this offer. I must listen down gopher holes and consult the stars for a sign. I shall burn prayer papers to the evil god of printers that he may whisper to me what manner of teeth this gift horse has."

"Just let me know," Ogden said.

"Ah, magic!" Hare said, helping himself to another drink. "With my wand I could make even you into a public benefactor, Sig. You will burn midnight oil only that others may enjoy gracious living. Words come to me — *noble* — *unselfish* — *magnanimous*. . . . That last one might be a bit heavy for the reading populace of Broken Wagon, though."

Ogden said brusquely, "I said to let me know."

Hare emptied his glass and stared at it. "A coincidence," he observed. "The interview and the drink have both come to an end." He put down the glass and started for the door.

Ogden said, "One minute. Here's a second offer. I happen to know that Miles paid you one hundred dollars a week. Presumably Bowman will keep you at the same price. You can continue to do the work and draw the pay, and I'll give you an additional fifty a week for your allegiance. Ask your printers' god how that sounds."

Hare puckered up his face again. Damn the man, Ogden thought; there was no reading him, no telling whether he was pleased. Hare said, "And you'll want to know what goes into the *Bugle* before any edition hits the camp?"

"Precisely."

"The spy's life is a romantic life," Hare said. "It is filled with cloaks and daggers and beautiful women. You appeal to the wild blood in me. I shall think it over."

Ogden wasn't sure whether he was being laughed at. He said quickly, "Of course I shall always claim that this conversation never took place."

Hare grinned and made his bow again. "Certainly," he said. "And tell Satterlee to forget it, too. Also, tell him that the next time he hides behind your curtain he must not stand so close that his big boot toes stick out."

Then he was gone.

Satterlee came from the bedroom, his broad face red. "Damn it, my boots weren't showing! He must have seen me come upstairs. He made a guess and bluffed." He dropped into the chair again and took a cigar from his pocket but did not light the weed. He began chewing on it.

Ogden said, "It's spilt milk, Kemp. I've warned you about being careless. What did you make of the talk?"

Satterlee said, "He didn't promise you anything. Not a thing. You gave out more than you got back, Sig. Seems like you made a mistake sending for him."

"We'll see," Ogden said. "He's a rogue at heart, and he'll remember the sound of money."

"Suppose he goes straight to Bowman?"

"That was the risk I took."

"Where's Bowman staying? Hotel?"

"Bar talk says he turned in at Helen Addison's. The miner who saw him figured that was news."

"Damned if it ain't!" Satterlee said. "Well, sooner or later some stranger was bound to see her room-for-rent sign and turn in there. The question is: will he stay when he hears about Jud?"

"He'll stay," Ogden decided and turned thoughtful again. "Kemp, maybe we're overlooking a possibility. Do you suppose word could be got to Jud Addison?"

Satterlee, too, became thoughtful. "I could put a couple of my boys hunting for him. But why bother? Sooner or later he'll show back. Sooner or later. And when he does, he'll find Bowman camping in his bed. Only I'm not for waiting. There's quicker ways of getting Bowman's hide tacked to the wall."

70

Ogden said, "Your trouble, Kemp, is that you think in terms of violence, always figuring that a man's body is most vulnerable. I'd like a look into Bowman's past. There might be something there that would send him packing."

Satterlee shook his head. "Nothing in our dicker says we got to operate alike. You go after Bowman your way; I'll go after him mine."

"Just be careful," Ogden said. "That's all I ask, Kemp. Be mighty careful."

CHAPTER FIVE

Man Running

Bowman got a coat for himself at the general store, which was also Broken Wagon's post office. He bought a sheepskin, but this one fitted him better. He took his time about making the purchase and looked over the rest of the stock in this littered place. High-piled shelves and counters held all the needs of the camp, including quick-made coffins, ladies' bonnets, and a churn. Bowman liked the varied smell of the place.

He had nothing to do until Miles Hascomb's funeral and no desire to loiter along Placer Street. Finally he took a chair in the store and read a week-old copy of the Great Falls *Tribune* that someone had discarded. A lot of excitement at Great Falls about the coming of the Manitoba Railroad; the new town had put on a big celebration when the happy day arrived. Very little in the paper about Sword-

Bearer; the scare that had since swept the territory had been only a rumour commanding small space when the paper had gone to press.

After an hour, Bowman glimpsed from the window what seemed to be a mass movement out on the street and went to the planking for a real look. People and carriages were wending to the west, but not in an orderly procession. He saw that the van had started up a road that twined to the top of the north slope. Far ahead was the flat-bed wagon bearing Hascomb's coffin. Bowman moved into the current of people and was carried along. The climb was one to put an ache in a man's ankles, and he wondered what possessed humanity that it so often placed its cemeteries at the tops of hills. Was this some groping towards the heaven the scriptures spoke about?

Broken Wagon's cemetery was new, numbering fewer than a score of graves. As yet no fence had been built around the scattered headboards. The flat-bed wagon had stopped beside a newly dug grave; the other wagons and carriages began pulling up close behind the improvised hearse, and the people wandered aimlessly among the graves.

Bowman found himself by a recent grave; in a tin can imbedded in the mound some withered flowers drooped. He read the marker: LUCIA WADSWORTH — BELOVED WIFE AND MOTHER — BORN NOVEMBER 15, 1864 — DIED SEPTEMBER 8, 1887. The bottom of the marker read: ANGELA WADSWORTH, INFANT DAUGHTER, and bore the lone, doom-shadowed date, September 8, 1887. Thus the tale was told. Walking Montana cemeteries, he'd often been struck by how young many people died. Women and children especially. Childbirth took its toll, and smallpox, and consumption. Another marker caught his eye. It said: CHONG LEE. No more than that. A hell of a long way from China, Bowman reflected.

He glimpsed Jenny Hascomb through the milling crowd. She was being helped from a carriage by Faro. The girl wore a black veil, and she'd put a coat over the dress she'd been wearing in the *Bugle* office. Faro stood close by her and was solemnly attentive. Had the girl all along been the real reason for Faro's interest in the Hascombs, Bowman wondered? No, Faro was far too old for Jenny.

Mrs. Addison was here, straight, pale,

and handsome; some cloaked girls who looked as though they might be from the hurdy-gurdy houses; and a great many miners. One wore a high plug hat and a fancy waistcoat, with a chain stretched across it that would have weighed down an ox. Rings blinked from his fingers. For all his finery, the man's whiskers were unkempt, and he had the gnarled look of a toiler. Some exchange of comment between two miners standing near Bowman told him he was seeing Sam Marble, founder of the camp.

Most of the men were armed, the holstered six-shooters showing plain; and one or two even carried rifles. This astonished Bowman, until he remembered the Indian scare. Did the fools think the redskins were going to attack a camp that was four thousand strong? And in broad daylight? Here on this peopled hill, the threat of Sword-Bearer seemed completely unreal. Couldn't anybody understand that civilisation had caught up with Montana? Hell, a telegraph line ran into this camp; and Helena, not far away, was sporting telephones and horse-drawn street cars these days. But fear didn't make any allowances for logic, and the fear in this crowd was an enlarged echo of the fear that had ridden the stagecoach last night. Miles Hascomb had died in an Indian attack, hadn't he?

Where, Bowman wondered, was the man who chewed cigars instead of smoking them?

A preacher had been recruited from somewhere, a bony, weathered man. Some circuit rider, Bowman supposed; he'd seen no church spire rising over Broken Wagon. The preacher had got at his work and was sawing away with his hands, his words booming out in the thin, mountain air. Bowman paid little attention. Words were no real comfort at such a time, and these didn't add anything in the way of solemnity. Bowman looked over his shoulder at the raw town stretched below, the farther slope, and the lifting mountains. Then he looked along this slope to the east and picked out Mrs. Addison's house. It was nearly the highest on the slope and stood apart from others, but there were a few shacks above it.

The preacher had fumbled open the Book, and Bowman listened then. The old words were worth a man's heeding. " 'I am the Resurrection, and the Life: he that believeth in Me, though he were dead, yet shall he live. . . .' "

Quite a promise that, and mighty comforting, Bowman thought. But Hascomb would want a newspaper in his heaven, and maybe a Sig Ogden handy to keep eternity exciting. Dull indeed it would be for a war horse like Miles to report only what this angel did, and that. "The Heavenly Hosts met last Tuesday, and it was decided that the golden streets should be given a spring sweeping. Gabriel was appointed chairman of a committee to provide brooms . . . St. Peter reports that almost twice as many people passed through the Pearly Gates this month as compared to the same period last year. Good luck, Pete."

Bowman shook his head, rebuking himself for his flippant thinking. Maybe a man shouldn't try to fathom the great mysteries.

" '. . . And whosoever liveth and believeth in Me shall never die. Believest thou this?' "

Not much snow here on the hilltop, Bowman noticed; the wind had swept it away. Wind rustled the sage and whimpered. To the west the sun was lowering behind the hills through which the stage had wended last night; the underbelly of the clouds was blood red, militantly fiery.

The preacher had closed the Book, his

work done. The box was being lowered, and someone had picked up a shovel. Faro helped Jenny back into the carriage. Had she wept? Her shoulders were firm, but she moved woodenly, as though she was very tired.

A man slouched up to the carriage and spoke to her — an old, lanky man in a rusty black suit. Those shoulders could have been bowed by leaning over a compositor's slate-topped table, and Bowman guessed that the fellow was Ben Hare. The crowd was fanning out like the spokes of a wheel; the ones afoot began to drift down the road, and the carriages were being turned about for the descent. The old man stepped away from the carriage; Jenny made a motion inviting him to ride, but the fellow shook his head and moved off.

Bowman manœuvred towards him. "You Ben Hare?"

The fellow gave him a quick look. He had sharp eyes in an old face. "Christened such," he said. "Benjamin Bartholomew Hare. It has the roll of thunder, don't you think? The only stranger who might be interested would be Neil Bowman."

Bowman fell in beside him. "I'd like to have a talk with you."

"It's a dry pastime," Hare observed. "Surely the occasion calls for a drink."

They were on to the slant. They walked along in silence until they hit the planks of Placer. Bowman said, "I'll buy the drink. Anywhere but the Imperial."

Hare's grin was crafty. "You black-listing them?"

Bowman smiled. "Haven't you heard? They're the opposition."

Hare shrugged. "Their whisky's good," he said, "provided you lay hands on the right bottle."

They turned in at the first saloon they came to. The place was smaller than the Imperial, but the dust rose as thick, and the bar seemed as crowded. Ben Hare wedged his way to the bar with the dexterity of long practice and asked for a bottle and glasses. Bowman paid for the liquor. The old printer toted it to a table in a far corner and sat down heavily. Only then did Bowman fully realise that Ben Hare was already carrying a great load of whisky. He judged that Hare was a man never completely sober, never completely drunk.

Hare sloshed liquor into the glasses and at once lifted his own. "Here's to a long and happy association," he proposed. "May our relationship be based upon a community of interests, an appreciation of good prose, and the common pursuit of the almighty dollar."

"You'll keep working for the *Bugle*, then?"

Hare emptied his glass, gave it an owlish look and promptly refilled it. "That, my young friend, is for you to say."

Bowman studied him, the feeling strong that he must know this man and know him well if his destiny was to be linked with Hare's. A deep one, Hare. A wise old badger, with cynicism on his tongue and in his eyes. But how much solid foundation did this man have?

Bowman asked, "What do I need to know about this camp?"

"First of all, the nature of one Jud Addison."

"Kin to Mrs. Addison?"

Hare nodded. "The news spread like the proverbial wildfire that you had taken up abode beneath that roof. Doubtless wagers are being laid as to how long you'll tarry there. Jud Addison is a man of fiery eye and mean disposition, and his moods are as black as his whiskers."

"I've seen his picture," Bowman said with sudden understanding. "Then she's not a widow?"

Hare shook his head. "No more than I."

"What about the man?"

"Jud is given to strong drink. Unlike you and me, he does not find conviviality in the cup; instead, it sets his feet upon destructive pathways. He celebrates his wrath by shooting up the town. Do you ask yourself what gnaws at a man when good whisky makes him murderous? In Jud's case, my guess is that the answer lies beneath that very roof under which you've chosen to bed. That's no concern of ours, though. Now and then Jud vanishes in an alcoholic haze. The trouble is, he likewise returns. Three weeks ago he went somewhere to bay at the moon. This has been his longest absence, and the Placer Street merchants are probably praying that the Indians have got him. A week ago, Mrs. Addison put out the shingle that drew your searching eye. But one of these squally days Jud will amble home. Do you follow me?"

"The hell with him," Bowman said.

Hare squinted, looking purely wicked. "I shall give you some fatherly advice. No, considering the difference in our years, I'll call it grandfatherly advice. Get the hell out from under Jud Addison's roof!"

"I can't," Bowman said. "Not now."

"Now what manner of asinine reasoning is that?"

"Obviously the town's waited to see what man would make the mistake of moving in. You've told me that the news has already spread that I am that man. If I move out now, people will know I've been warned, won't they, and chose to play safe. It would cost me face in the camp. It would cost the *Bugle* face. So it would be a victory for Sig Ogden."

Hare looked immensely amused. "Better a dead lion than a live coward? Now there's a philosophy for fools, I must say! I wouldn't have pegged you for a simpleton. Jenny and Faro were telling me that you bought into Miles's fight against Ogden lock, stock, and barrel. Perhaps you did — perhaps you did. But what I'd like to know is what's in it for you."

Bowman said, "I hate any man who throws Ogden's kind of shadow. But when I pinch him, it will be where it hurts him most — in the purse."

Hare sloshed more whisky into his glass. Not looking at Bowman, he said very casually, "Excuse me changing the subject, but we've got headline news for the next edition. Came over the telegraph wire this morning. Bart Carney slugged a guard, got through Deer Lodge's gate, and is on the loose. Now what do you make of that?"

Bowman felt the chair scrape under him and realised that he'd jerked. His first fierce thought was that he must not let his face betray him. Not for a second must this discerning old devil see how hard the news had hit him. He forced his voice to the same casual tone Hare had used. "Carney is the stuff from which headlines are made, Ben. King outlaw of them all — a legend, if you like. Certainly we'll give it space."

Hare stared at him with real admiration. "God!" he said. "I'd hate to play poker with you!"

Bowman shoved back his chair. "I'd better be getting along."

Hare grinned. "To look for the fastest horse you can buy?"

Anger rose in Bowman, and he was done with sparring. "Damn it, what kind of bluff do you think you're running?"

"That's a good question," Hare said. "Do you know the Yankee trick of answering a question by asking another? Tell me this then: when you were dickering with Miles, didn't he remember your name?"

Bowman drew in a breath and expelled

it. "At the last, yes."

"Miles didn't do much of our typeset-ting," Hare said. "That exalted labour fell to me. When you pick out the news a letter at a time, you remember it. The item was small and came along about the time of our first edition in the spring. As a reward for good behaviour, one Neil Bowman was being allowed beyond the wall of the Territorial pen to learn a trade for which he'd shown some aptitude. You were to work on the *New Northwest* in Deer Lodge town, reporting back to the pen each night. We get an exchange copy of that news-paper. Your name appeared in it more than once last summer."

"You've told Hascomb's girl this?"

Hare grinned slyly. "Not yet. If you're half a rogue, Bowman, and I'm half a rogue, together we make a whole rogue. I've worked a lot of years at the beck and call of men who presumed they were my betters. Some of them were, too. Miles, for instance. But I've waited for the main chance. Maybe it's come. When you get around to pinching at Ogden's purse, you're going to cut me in for half. We're partners, friend."

Bowman stood up. "And why did you mention Bart Carney?"

"To see how far out of your skin you'd jump. Our files don't go back many months, so I got on the telegraph wire and checked with Helena. You hail from the Yellowstone country. You were charged with mavericking and sentenced to ten years in the pen. While you were there, you were Bart Carney's cell mate. You were pardoned about two weeks ago. Now everybody knows that the loot was never recovered from the stage robbery that sent Carney up for twenty years. And you came out of the hills with a saddlebag full of mouldy currency. Thing that puzzles me is how he happened to tell you where he hid it."

"And to see how I'd react, you ran a bluff about his escaping?"

Hare grinned again. "Nary bluff." He swept his arm in a vast semicircle. "He's out there somewhere, and he's on the move."

Bowman turned and walked from the saloon. Dusk had fallen, and he stood on the planking. The cool breeze was a kindness, for in him was a rising fever, a feeling that he should be running. He steadied himself with an effort. Careful! he thought; panic could make him reckless. Only one thing was certain — he had to be gone from here. He forced himself to cross over to the restaurant where he'd eaten earlier to-day and have another meal. He took his time at eating and asked that a package of cold meat and bread be made up for him. After that he found a livery stable and dickered for a saddle horse. He had to pay two hundred dollars for a roan gelding, but he didn't argue. Besides the five thousand he'd paid to Jenny Hascomb from the saddlebag, he'd had other money which he'd carried in his pockets. Buying the horse took nearly the last of it.

He led the horse as far as the stage station and got his own saddle and put it on the roan. Deep dark had come, and the camp was just awakening to its boisterous night life. Sound spilled from the Imperial, a blend of piano music and the voices of men; and the wash of lamps lay yellow upon the planking all up and down Placer. He mounted and rode to the proper cross street and turned up the slope towards Mrs. Addison's. Only one last thing left now — to get his saddlebag.

He could only walk the roan on the slope, yet he was a man running just the same. He was not ashamed of the fear that was driving him to the far trails. He even felt grateful to Ben Hare for telling him of

Carney's escape and so giving him this slight margin. Then the thought struck him that Hare might have been playing a more devious game than he, Bowman, had thought. Suppose that talk about being half a rogue and looking for the main chance had been only talk. Suppose Hare actually possessed some deep-seated loyalty to the Hascombs that had made him contrive to drive Neil Bowman out of Broken Wagon and thus out of the *Bugle*'s future, for Jenny's sake. Bowman thought then of looking for Jenny and asking for the return of his five thousand dollars. But was there time?

Off Placer, he was in a region of darkness and silence that tilted upwards, with the outline of the Addison place looming above. Once over the top of the hill, he'd lose himself in the night and the timber and the snow. Again he considered seeing the Hascomb girl first, and then he heard the scream. It rose in anguish and terror out of the night and broke off abruptly in a vast, stricken sigh.

Bowman spurred the roan. Men up here on the slope, a knot of men that fell apart as he came charging upon them. A gun sounded, the flame smearing a red swathe against the darkness. He got his own gun out and fired. Down on Placer, someone shouted, aroused by the gunfire. One of those shadowy figures here on the hillside ran at Bowman and tried to haul him from his saddle. He struck at the man with his gun barrel. Another came at him, and he was hauled from the horse. Men closed in upon him, and he fought. He gripped at greasy buckskin but could get no fast hold. How many men here? A half-dozen? He couldn't be sure. But when his flailing gun barrel wrung an ejaculation of pain out of one of them, terror struck through him. These were Indians! He imagined he heard more shouting down the slope and perhaps the slogging of boots. He glimpsed a lantern bobbing below. One with whom he struggled struck at him with something heavy, the blow numbing his shoulder. Then pain came, washing through him. He got hold of the fellow's wrist and bent the Indian's arm down, and a gun in the Indian's hand exploded harmlessly. But in its glare Bowman got a glimpse of Indian faces, high planed, obsidian eyed, and coppery; and he saw something else.

A man lay sprawled upon the ground face up, the top of his head a raw and ugly wound where his scalp had been lifted.

This, then, had been the one who'd screamed, and screaming, died. He wore a sheepskin coat, and it was the coat Bowman recognised. Here was the nameless person who'd said he slept in a shack far up this north slope. Here was a man who'd died because he'd worn Neil Bowman's coat and taken Bowman's path. Knowing this with a sudden, terrible certainty, Bowman felt himself pressed backward and downward by the sheer weight of the men against him.

CHAPTER SIX

Blocked Trail

His second certainty was as terrifying as the first. He was going to die here, just as the other man had died. Whoever was coming up the slope — that lantern seemed to be bobbing nearer — would come too late. Bowman went down, and one of the Indians fell across him. Rolling over, Bowman shed the man and struggled to his feet, but he'd lost his gun. He felt hands pulling at him, and again someone got in a blow at his shoulder with a gun barrel, but it was a quiet knife he really feared. The heavy sheepskin deflected some of the blows, but he was sweating hard. He broke free by a mighty effort and tried clearing a path for himself with swinging fists. No blow seemed to land where he aimed it. At least five men against him, he knew now. They came at him again.

He shouted; the sound seemed feeble.

Damn it, what was holding back the men on the lower slope?

Then, above him at the Addison place, the front door opened, and a splash of light fell out upon the snow. Bowman heard a scream, not the anguished death scream of the man who'd gone down under a scalping knife but the high-pitched scream of a woman. He glimpsed the silhouette of Mrs. Addison in her doorway. Such a small thing as that scream was the saving of him. Probably the Indians feared that people might come pouring from the house and trap them between such a force and the one coming up the slope. Or possibly the scream simply unnerved them. Suddenly their charge broke; moccasins slithered in the night; and his attackers were gone, scurrying off into the shadows.

He stood reeling, his chest afire from exertion, his breath sobbing in his throat. He got down on his hands and knees and felt around for his lost gun and quickly found it. He lifted the gun and peered into the darkness and fired at one of the fleeing savages. He was standing with the gun held poised when a dozen miners spilled around him and a lantern shone on his face. Questions beat at him, but he only shook his head, not yet having the breath for talk.

The light fell this way and that and picked up the man on the ground.

Someone cried shrilly, "My god! Scalped!"

Bowman saw fear hit them. He had never thought fear could be so nearly tangible, but it stood out that plain now. Like those in the stagecoach last night, these men had lived in expectation of something like this; and now it had happened, here in the camp. It was rumour turned into actuality. There was that dead man lying in the lantern light. On the fringe of this knot of men, someone retched and became very sick. Another, made of harder material, demanded of Bowman what the hell had happened here.

Bowman told them, making it short. He'd heard a scream and come just too late. He'd made a fight, and there might have been two dead men on the ground if the Indians hadn't cut for cover. He said nothing about the other man's wearing his sheepskin. He wanted time to think about that.

The miner who had put the question to Bowman now appointed himself leader. He flashed the lantern full upon the dead man and said, "Carry him out of here," his face harsh and angry. "We'd best get the word around. No sleep for a lot of us to-night. This camp's got to have a ring of sentries."

Someone had caught up Bowman's horse and put the reins in his hands. Nobody, he noticed, was making any move to go off questing the shadows for the Indians. He didn't blame them for their reluctance. He shouldered away, leading the roan, and moved on up to the house. Mrs. Addison still stood in the open doorway. He tied the horse to a small bush and came into the parlour. Mrs. Addison closed the door behind him. She stood looking at him, and he asked, "Do you own a gun?"

She nodded.

"Get it and lay it here on the table where it will be handy," he said. "When you go to bed, keep it close by. Those were Indians. They knifed and scalped a man. If you hadn't opened the door when you did, they would have knifed and scalped me, too."

He hadn't meant to be so brutally abrupt, but she took the news more calmly than any man out there, even the one who had appointed himself leader. For a moment her handsome face was startled. Her bosom lifted and fell, her lips drew straight, and her eyes showed a faint shadow, but she spoke calmly. "I thought I heard a scream. When I listened hard, there were shots and a sound like scuffling. Then I heard you shout." She looked him full in the eye and her voice turned remote. "Who was the man they killed?"

"Some bummer," he said. "Nobody in that bunch of miners seemed to know him."

He couldn't tell whether this news pleased or displeased her. She said, shrugging, "I'll get that gun."

Reaction was beginning to hit him from the bout out there on the slope. He thought he knew why this woman had been alert to sounds and why she had to know who had died. How many nights had she awaited Jud Addison's footfall? But his nerves were too tightly drawn to allow him tolerance, and he said with an edge to his voice, "You're mighty calm about the whole thing! Do you think that not even a marauding Indian would dare enter Jud Addison's house?"

She had turned towards her own bedroom. She swung back and made a small gesture with her hands. "So you've been told about Jud," she said. "And you're thinking that I should have been the one to tell you. It never crosses Jud's mind, when he takes himself off, that I must live while he's gone. Renting out a room was a necessity. If I'd warned you about him, you might have turned away."

"I'm sorry," he said.

He could have told her now that he was quitting this house and this camp to-night, but he didn't. Let all of them find out he was gone only when he turned up missing. Let them even guess, if they liked, that Indians had got him. It might serve to throw Bart Carney off his trail. He walked into the kitchen and climbed the short flight of stairs. He got out the key to his bedroom door; but when he put it to the lock, the door gave under his hand and swung inward.

He stood then with fear cold in his stomach, a fear as strong as that he'd known during the attack but of a different kind. He lunged into the room and got down on his knees and groped under the bed. The saddlebag was gone.

He stood up. He walked to the dresser and got the lamp burning, lifted it, and had a good look around. No sign of disturbance here; the room seemed just as he had left it. He examined the door. The jamb was splintered, and he judged that the lock had been forced by a crowbar. He put the lamp back upon the dresser and blew it out. He stood in the darkness and found that his hands had formed fists. This last catastrophe was the greatest that had struck him to-day, but as he fitted it in with the rest, he began to see the shape of a pattern. From this came an angry conviction.

He came back down to the parlour and found Helen Addison still there. She was seated now, and an old Army Model Colt .44 lay upon the table beside her sewing basket. He said, "My door was forced. I've been robbed."

This truly startled her. She came out of the chair, a hand rising to her cheek. "No!"

"You can look for yourself. The lock is broken."

She shook her head. "Then I made it easy for them. I forgot to lock the front door when I went to the funeral this afternoon. I remembered by the time I'd walked halfway across the hilltop to the cemetery, but I didn't turn back. I have nothing worth stealing. What did they take from you?"

"Everything," he said. She looked so troubled that he came and put his hands on her shoulders. "I'm not blaming you." His anger rose again. "I've got to go now and see a man."

He let himself out the front door and climbed upon the roan. He told himself that he mustn't let his anger colour his judgment or make his hand unsteady, but still the conviction he'd reached in the ravaged room stood out clearly. Below, the bell began beating in the tower, and the sound startled him. His first frantic thought was that the Indians had fired the camp, but at once he realised that he was hearing no strident alarm but a slower tolling; likely the bell was calling Broken Wagon to assembly.

He rode down through the darkness to Placer and came upon a street drained of raucousness; light still splashed from the saloons, but men were moving in tight little knots along the planking, and there was no feel of revelry. He saw the glint of lamplight on rifle barrels. Light shone from the window of the *Bugle*'s office, and before the building he found Jenny and Ben Hare standing.

He reined up. Jenny had on the coat she had worn at the funeral, but Hare had swapped his rusty suit for the leather apron of his trade. The man had been working, Bowman realised, and maybe the girl had, too. He found this surprising until he remembered the realistic philosophy with which she had ordered the funeral held at once.

Hare twisted up his old face with his wicked grin and said, "I see you got yourself a horse. Looks fast, too."

Bowman took a perverse pleasure in saying, "I'll be here to-morrow morning, Ben. Ready to go to work."

Jenny said, "We heard it was you they jumped. I'm glad you came off whole skinned." She said this with no real show of emotion, yet she sounded sincere.

Bowman nodded. "It was that bummer who was wearing the coat I gave away."

Jenny drew in her breath sharply.

"That's what I thought, too," Bowman said dryly.

"The whole camp is getting armed and ready now," Jenny said. "Maybe it's best. Maybe the man who went up that slope would have been killed no matter what coat he'd been wearing."

"Maybe," Bowman said. "But I don't think so."

She was not afraid, he noticed. She stood deep in thought, biting her lip. She was as brave as Mrs. Addison had been, but it was a different courage, a kind based on the weighing of facts. For the first time he saw her as Miles Hascomb's daughter;

there was more than an echo of the man in this girl. And he saw, too, that the difference between her and Helen Addison was like the difference between Miles Hascomb and Faro last night. There was a thinker's courage and a fatalist's courage.

He nudged his horse.

"Be careful," Jenny called.

He lifted his hand, including Ben Hare in the salute. The printer was staring at him, puzzled. Bowman rode across Placer to the rack before the Imperial, dismounted and tied up his horse, and strode into the saloon.

A lot of men were here. They jammed the bar and sat at the tables, and the ground dust from their boots still filled the air. But this might have been a wake. They were a silent, scared bunch, buying courage out of bottles. Sam Marble was among them, declaiming at the bar. Bowman saw Faro at a table; the gambler looked up and recognised him and gave him the slightest of nods. Bowman was heading straight towards the stairs Ogden had indicated when he'd suggested this afternoon that they go to his office and talk business. Bowman got to the bottom of the stairs before a bartender came from behind the counter and loomed up to block his way.

"You can't go up there," the bartender said.

Bowman hit him twice. His first blow was to the man's midriff and doubled him over; the second caught the fellow under the chin and straightened him. Then the man's legs folded and he sat down heavily. Bowman climbed the stairs.

He came bursting into Ogden's office to find Ogden sitting in a captain's chair before his desk. The man's bony face revealed his surprise as Bowman banged the door shut behind him, but only for an instant was Ogden caught off guard. He smiled faintly at Bowman. "I hope," he said, "that I'm not the last to congratulate you on your escape to-night. The tale has already travelled the camp."

Bowman said, "Never mind that kind of talk. Where have you got it?"

"Got what?"

"My saddlebag. You can keep it for a souvenir. But I want the money and the paper I was carrying in it."

Ogden shrugged his thin shoulders, his face utterly innocent. "I don't know what you're talking about."

Bowman had to admire the man's great aplomb, but this didn't lessen his anger. He crossed the room and swept aside the curtain at the bedroom doorway. Mighty fancy fixings in this place! The adjoining room was carpeted with a rug rich as the one in the office, and the high-backed bed was of mahogany, but it was a small iron safe in the corner that interested Bowman. He tugged at the handle and found the safe locked.

He stepped back into the office and brought out his gun.

"Come and open it," he ordered.

Ogden said calmly, "You'll find nothing in that safe that belongs to you. Take my solemn word for it."

Bowman stood defeated. He was remembering the bartender who had moved so quickly to block his way. He nodded. "No, you probably wouldn't keep what you stole where I might force my way to it. You knew damn' well I'd come rampaging up here." He holstered his gun.

Ogden smiled. "Now you're being sensible."

Bowman picked up a chair, swung it around, straddled it, and leaned his folded arms upon the back. He stared at Ogden. "Just the same," Bowman said, "we're having a talk."

Ogden brought a watch out of his pocket and had a look at it. "I can give you about ten minutes," he said. "Such miners as aren't already out on patrol duty are gathering in my bar for a mass meeting about the Indian situation. I'm to address them."

"God!" Bowman said. "How much cheek can a man have?"

Ogden pocketed the watch. "Say what you've got to say. And you might as well be comfortable meanwhile. There's liquor on the sideboard."

"*You*'ll need the bracer, when you hear me out," Bowman said. "Some Indians waited at the stage station last night. Where they came from, I don't know; but I saw Indians here when I first got to the camp, and they could have been hired for a bottle apiece. The point is that they were waiting for the stagecoach. Or, to go a step farther, they were waiting for one of the passengers. Miles Hascomb. They got him, too. That was a smart way to cover up a murder. The whole country is jumpy over this Sword-Bearer scare. Indians attack, and a man is killed. Too bad! What you didn't figure on, Sig, was Hascomb's selling half his paper to one of the other passengers last night."

Ogden raised a hand to pluck at the shawl about his shoulders. "No," he said carefully, "who'd have guessed that would happen?"

"You offered to buy me out. I wouldn't sell. This afternoon, while the Addison house was empty, you had my room forced. You got my money. You got something else, too — a paper in my saddlebag that shows that Governor Leslie pardoned me from the penitentiary."

Ogden pursed his lips. "A pardon? So you were speaking of yourself when you told me of the man who'd been framed into Deer Lodge."

"Of course," Bowman said. "Now about that money: I don't think it interested you greatly. Probably you thought that if I found myself broke I'd take your offer to buy the *Bugle*. More likely you hoped you'd find something incriminating to give you a wedge against me. You found no such thing, but you've hidden out the money so it won't incriminate *you*. The main point is that once you realised you had nothing to use against me, you decided on another step. Right?"

"Go on," Ogden said tonelessly. "You interest me."

"Some Indians waited on the slope to-night. The same Indians, I'd guess, who waited for a shot at Miles. What had worked once could work again. With this Indian scare, let a man be found scalped, and who'd ask questions? Those Indians were told to wait for a man of about my height and wearing a sheepskin who'd be coming up the slope to the Addison place. Some bummer lived in a shack up beyond Addisons'. This afternoon I gave him my coat. He's the one that's dead."

"Yes — ?" Ogden said.

"That's all. I want that money back, Sig."

"And what would you have done with it if you hadn't lost it?"

"Somewhere I'd have bought a piece of land and the beginning of a cow herd. It was my future I was carrying in that saddle-bag."

"I'm sorry for you," Ogden said. "But you're barking up the wrong tree." He leaned back in his chair and brought his finger tips together, forming a steeple. He looked satisfied, sure of himself.

Again Bowman realised that he must not let anger unsteady him. He stood up. He said in an even voice, "You damn' fool, you twisted your own twine when you stole that money. I bought a horse this evening. It's tied up out front right now. An hour ago I was headed for Addisons' to get my saddlebag and be over the hill and gone from here. Now my trail is blocked. Do you understand? I'd be out of here by now. You'd have been done with me. Give me my money and I'll still be gone."

Ogden shook his head, smiling faintly. "If I had your money — *if*, mind you — and were to hand it over, it would be the same as admitting to the truth of every wild guess you've made. I'd really be the fool you've named me, Bowman."

"Then my future is here," Bowman said. "All that's left me is my half interest in the *Bugle*. And that's my club against you."

Ogden said thoughtfully, "I'm curious as to why you suddenly decided to clear out of here."

Bowman shook his head. He wondered what would happen if he told Ogden that Bart Carney might be riding this way and that Carney, too, would be interested in the whereabouts of that saddlebag. He'd like to see Ogden's face if he blurted out that this camp was now comparatively safe for Neil Bowman, since, when the chips were down, Carney's interest would be in the money rather than in the man who carried it off. But the revelation was a luxury he couldn't afford, not with one as wily as Sig Ogden.

Bowman turned towards the door. "All

you need to know is that you've made me into a newspaperman. I'll give you good reading in the *Bugle*. Good-night, Sig."

CHAPTER SEVEN

All the Old Days

When he came back to the house on the slope, the door was barred and he had to thump for admittance. Mrs. Addison swung the bar into place again when she had let him in.

He had put up the roan at the livery stable where he had bought the horse, and had walked up from Placer. He'd climbed that lane of darkness where so recently death had waited, and had climbed warily, though he hadn't truly expected that the shadows would be peopled again. He had been certain that his deductions about what had happened earlier this evening were correct — so certain that he knew Ogden would not have ordered the lightning to strike twice in the same place. Moreover, there were guards strung out through the camp now. One had challenged Bowman just before he reached the door.

Inside the house, he looked down at his boots. "Sorry to be dragging in mud."

He was breathing heavily from anger and exertion. He'd levelled a new challenge at Ogden, but he had no sense of triumph. Instead he felt trapped, forced into a course of action different from that of his choosing an hour or so ago.

Mrs. Addison said, "I have coffee on the stove. Would you like some?"

He nearly refused. She, too, was a conspirator, playing her own small and subtle game; she had snared him with that sign she had placed on her house. But he could not really think of her as an enemy, not when he remembered how frankly she had spoken of her plight. Still, he wasn't quite comfortable with her.

"Coffee — ?" he said. He nodded.

She left the room, moving in her sinuous fashion. He sat down and felt the eyes of Jud Addison on him from the crayon portrait. As long as that damn' picture was there, Addison was all over the house. In his mind he told Jud Addison to go to hell. Mrs. Addison came back and placed coffee before him. It was steaming, and he waited for it to cool. When he finally took a sip, he made a face.

"I laced it with whisky," she said.

"You've had quite an evening."

He was grateful to her. Twice grateful, remembering how her appearance at the doorway had tipped the scales for him when he had fought those Indians. It prickled his skin just to think of that fight. He said, "When I first arrived in Broken Wagon, I saw a few Indians sitting in front of one of the saloons. Are there many in camp?"

"None, really," she said. "Those were probably Piegans you saw. Some of the young bucks jump the reservation occasionally and wander around. I've heard that a few of them have been working for cattle outfits over in the Twosleep, across the hump. They stay for a week or a month and then move on. The Indian agent never bothers his head about them as long as they're not making trouble. In due time they always come drifting back to the reservation."

Like Jud Addison comes drifting home, he thought. He sipped at his coffee again. Mrs. Addison had seated herself and picked up her sewing. He watched her. She seemed out of place here in Broken Wagon. She had been born to gentler surroundings and carried some aura of better places with her. By what queer destiny had she become attached to that whiskered ape on the wall? And why had she stayed with him through his drunkenness and his wildness? Then he remembered Ben Hare's hint that the woman was the cause of Addison's furies. Bowman shook his head. He didn't want to believe that. Lamplight gave a sheen to her brass-yellow hair, and the sadness he had observed earlier still showed on her face. It had been there a long time, he judged.

His eyes roved the room. This house was better than a man would expect to find in a boom camp. Much better. The organ against the wall had been freighted a long way, and the worn rug had once cost a pretty penny. Addison must have located one of the richer claims or have owned a hefty stake when he arrived. Bowman shook off this thinking; such matters were no concern of his.

He finished his coffee and rose abruptly. "I'm going to bed," he said.

She looked up. "Wait. There is something I must say. When I placed that sign outside, I didn't intend to take in just any stranger. You are here by my choice, Neil. While you were deciding whether you wanted the room, I was deciding whether I wanted you in it."

"And what settled your choice for you?"

She shrugged. "Who knows? A woman's intuition, perhaps. Or maybe it was the fact that you were interested in Jud's picture as a piece of handiwork. Otherwise you would not have stared so long."

"That proved nothing," he said. "I'm only a rough man who's grown rougher with the years." And then, because the whole camp might soon know it anyway, now that the knowledge belonged to both Ben Hare and Sig Ogden, he said, "I'm fresh out of Deer Lodge prison."

She merely nodded. "Aren't all of us serving time in one sort of prison or another? I still don't regret choosing you."

She smiled at him warmly, intimately; and he felt himself shy from her. He went up to his room and closed the door. The moon had risen, and he looked out on the snowy slope just below his window ledge. He thought of the self-appointed sentries walking the night and debated about that ravaged door. He expected no attack on himself, but still there was Ogden's enmity to remember. After all, the lightning *might* strike twice. He propped a chair under the door knob. Without lighting the lamp, he undressed and climbed into bed. He lay flat upon his back with his fingers locked

111

at the nape of his neck.

Sleep didn't come to him. He'd slept this afternoon, and there hadn't been enough whisky in his coffee to make him drowsy. Pictures began chasing one another through the turmoil of his mind. He had dug deep into his past to-day in his talks with both Ben Hare and Sig Ogden, and in his thinking. He remembered what he had told Ogden in their afternoon encounter in the Imperial, and he could see himself in that Yellowstone Valley courtroom again with the jury filing in and that red-whiskered cattleman sitting well to the front. "Ten years," the judge had said, burying those two words under a lot of fancy ones that didn't take any part of the sting away. And old Sherm Wheeler had sat there combing his red beard with his fingers and hiding his smile behind his hand. Two years dead now, old Sherm was, but that didn't lessen Bowman's hate any.

The worst thing had not been having the ten years loaded on his shoulders, he remembered. Not that afternoon he had stood facing the judge. The worst thing had been to stand there in the court looking like a thief before men who had been his neighbours. And the hardest thing had been to see the sudden flare of triumph in old Sherm Wheeler's eyes.

Later, when he had gone handcuffed to a deputy to Deer Lodge pen, he had begun to realise how heavy ten years could be. Twenty he was at the time, and thirty he would be when he got out. Young yet, he had tried to tell himself, yet thirty seemed a ripe old age when he was twenty and prison loomed ahead. A man had only so many years — three score and ten, the Book said — and these were golden coins not to be spent heedlessly. And here were ten of them being flung to the crying wind.

Something had died in him then. Some humour had gone out of him, and some tolerance.

He hadn't known how Deer Lodge would look. He thought of dank, grey walls and echoing corridors along which shadowy men walked as they had in the books his mother had got for him in his boyhood. All prisons in his mind had thus become a composite of the Bastille Dr. Manette had known, the prisons of Defoe's day, and the old Tower of London. But the first sight of Deer Lodge Valley, framed by the high reaches of Mount Powell and a ring of pine-clad hills, had seemed beautiful. Even with the iron on his wrists, it had seemed beautiful. And the prison had at least been a surprise.

No moat and clanking drawbridge here. Not that he had really expected such; he had just had no true imagining at all. A mighty primitive place, this Territorial penitentiary which was being run as a federal institution by contract. Thirteen years it had been standing — a couple of small two-story stone cellhouses, an office and a small waiting room. Some frame and log buildings sat deep in the yard. A high log palisade surrounded the prison. He thought of Fenimore Cooper's tales when he had seen that encircling fence. Sentry boxes stood at each corner of the palisade, with rifle-toting guards in them. Later he had learned that the sentry boxes were empty at night, when the prisoners were locked in their cells.

Well, he was far enough from Deer Lodge now. He stirred restlessly in the bed. Moonlight came through the window and laid a rectangle of light upon the floor, and he heard quiet movement somewhere in the house and, listening, judged that Helen Addison was going to bed. He kicked at the covers and wished that he could sleep. God, but it did no good, turning over all the old days in his mind! How deep were they grooved into him, that he could not shake loose from them?

A first prison year, and a second. A man fighting against the dull, grey, endless routine, but making that fight only in his mind, because the one chance that any of the golden coins might be spared him lay in good behaviour and so in the hope of pardon or parole. A third year, with the bitterness a slow boil in him and the feeling growing that he had been cheated and thus was running up a debt to collect from the outside world. Wild yearnings had begun to plague him that third year. How would it feel to be in a saddle again? How would the Yellowstone look from the rimrock above Billings? And where were the friends who'd written during the first couple of years but got out of the habit because he was someone dead and buried as far as the outside world was concerned?

Then they moved him into Bart Carney's cell. An old lifer had died and been toted to the prison section of Hillcrest Cemetery, and so Neil Bowman had been moved.

He had known Carney casually from his own first days in the pen. Carney had already been there a couple of years, sweating out that twenty-year stretch they had given him for armed robbery. Carney was the man pointed out to every new prisoner, the he-wolf who commanded awe and respect because of the legend he had made of himself. Yes, they had told it mighty scary about Bart Carney. For twenty years every unsolved crime in the Territory had been laid to him. A he-wolf, indeed; and he had even looked like one, lean, grey, and sharp-featured, and walking light.

That first night Bowman had stretched himself out in the bottom bunk so recently occupied by the old lifer. Carney had got hold of him by the ankles and dumped him to the floor. Hard. Mighty hard. Carney had said, "I'm taking this bunk. Climb aloft, boy."

Bowman had picked himself up and come at Carney then. His charge had been urged by anger, and something else, too — a realisation that he might have to share this tiny square of space with this man for many years. Whatever their relationship was to be, it would be determined this first night. He had got his arms around Carney and wrestled him across the cell, the two of them panting and straining. Carney was all wire and rawhide, a hard man to hold on to; but he was nearly fifty, and Bowman had had the advantage of youth. Still, it had been quite a tussle. They had fought in silence, mindful that they must not bring the guards upon them. At last Bowman had pinned the outlaw upon the floor, holding him there till Carney quit struggling.

"Do I take the lower bunk?" Bowman had demanded in a fierce whisper.

"She's all yours," Carney had said.

Bowman had let him up, then climbed to the upper bunk. "You're a lot older than I am," he said. "I can do the climbing."

They had been friends from there on out, Bowman recalled. Nothing warm about it, though! just a kind of understanding between them and once in a while a tobacco sack shared when either of them was low on the makings. Maybe it had been an armed truce rather than a friendship. But sometimes Carney had talked the long nights away, spinning tales of the outlaw trail that stretched from Canada to Mexico.

He had been a smart one, Carney, making friends at hard-scrabble ranches so there was always a ready horse for him. Once he had talked about the hold-up that had put him inside for twenty years. He mentioned the loot he had buried and how the Territory had tried to make a dicker with him, promising him a lighter sentence if he would tell where he had stashed the stolen money. None of that for yours truly, Bart Carney. At least he had him a stake when the gates finally swung wide.

And that night he had talked in his sleep.

Just a murmur at first. Something about a big rock being shaped like an Indian's head, with the war feathers sticking up. "Sight from nose . . . old Indian," Carney had muttered. "West . . . lightning-struck pine . . ." Then an incoherent mumble.

"How far from the pine tree?" Bowman asked gently.

"Got to dig," Carney said thickly.

"How far from the pine tree?" Bowman insisted.

"Twenty long paces — north."

It had been a night such as this one, a night when Bowman couldn't sleep. He had heard that if you fed questions to a sleep talker, his mind would supply answers. That night he tried it, out of boredom, but suddenly he was caught up in rising excitement. That money could be his!

He guessed quickly enough what was making Carney talk. Carney had hidden his loot with the thought that he might be caught and thus might not be able to get back to his cache for a long time. Maybe he had taken such a precaution after many a robbery. Wise old wolf that he was, he had memorised the location of his hiding-place so there would be nothing in writing to fall into the wrong hands. But twenty years was a long time for a man to have to remember. Carney must have repeated the directions to himself many times in his waking hours, wanting them set tight. Sight from the nose of the rock shaped like an Indian's head — due west to a lightning-blasted pine — then dig twenty long paces due north from the tree.

That night he had been telling of the hold-up and so had got his mind on the buried loot. And he had gone to sleep concerned with the things he must remember.

Bowman got all of it bit by bit. Where in the wide world was this rock like an Indian's head? Finding out took a lot of questioning, since most of the answers were senseless mumbles. The starting place was Helena, and from there a man had to take the road towards Whitewater Gulch. The name of a ranch must be remembered, too — the Muleshoe. There was an old mining road leading south from the Muleshoe. . . .

Now and again the answers had come so

clear and prompt that he'd wondered if Carney was awake and stringing him along, making a game of pretending to be supplying information. Even when Bowman had ridden from Helena to the Muleshoe months later and taken the road south, his eye peeled for that Indian-like rock, he hadn't been sure. Not till he had seen the rock and found the lightning-blasted pine and felt the scrape of his shovel against that green Wells Fargo treasure box. Not till he had stripped the protective wrappers from the bundles of currency inside. . . .

But many days had dropped from the calendar before he made that ride, days in which he'd known a growing fever to be free. Now there was twenty thousand dollars waiting beyond the wall. Enough for a new start. Enough to buy cattle to stock any piece of land he might settle on. His Yellowstone place had been sold for taxes to Sherm Wheeler and now belonged to Wheeler's heirs. Old Sherm hadn't got much good out of what he'd acquired by planting a worked-over hide in Neil Bowman's barn, but the place was lost to Bowman just the same. Damned if a man didn't have something coming to him to replace what had been lost! At least he had kept telling himself that, whenever he got thinking too strongly that Carney's buried loot didn't belong to him any more than it did to Carney.

That was when the first tussling had begun between the man he had once been and the man he had become. That was when he had decided he could not afford softness, not ever again.

The Deer Lodge newspaper job had given him a chance at escape. He had got the job because the prisoners had wanted a petition drawn up over some grievance, and Bowman had worded the petition for them, making it persuasive. The warden had seemed more impressed by the preamble than by the long list of signatures. He had talked to Bowman many times after that, and one day Bowman had been called into the office and offered a proposition. The warden had made a dicker with the *New Northwest* so that Bowman could work for that newspaper.

"You're no run-of-the-mine convict," the warden had said. "I think you deserve a chance to learn something that can be useful to you. What's more, I've looked into the affair that got you sent here. It smells like a frame. I'm not promising you anything, and I don't want to get your hopes high; but next time I'm in Helena, I'm going to talk to Governor Leslie. He's new, a lawyer out of Kentucky who should be able to see the holes in the court testimony against you. Perhaps a pardon can be arranged."

Thus hope had sustained Bowman while he had gone each day into Deer Lodge town and done his work on the newspaper. He had liked the job, and he'd had a chance to try his hand at a lot of phases of it — setting type, writing news stories, taking a turn at the hand press — but he had been haunted by the notion that all he had to do was keep walking some day when he was out on an errand, keep walking till he sighted that rock shaped like an Indian's head. But each night he'd faithfully returned to the prison and the waiting cell. When he took the long walk, he wanted to walk free; and he had at last, with the governor's pardon in his pocket alongside money he had earned on the *New Northwest*, money enough to buy a horse and some gear and a shovel.

That was the way it had been. The only bad luck had been in losing his horse in the hills the other night and finding himself afoot in the cold that might have taken his life. He could hark up again the irony of walking along the road and thinking of the warmth and shelter of Deer Lodge. But the stage had come, the stage that was to have borne him on a first lap towards another range, where he would have looked for a piece of land.

Then Miles Hascomb had come into his life and gone out of it, and everything had been changed. Just because Sig Ogden had cast the same blighting shadow as Sherm Wheeler. Or was there more to it than that? He didn't know, and probably it did not matter now. Not after the news Ben Hare had given him — the news that Bart Carney had got shed of Deer Lodge and was on the prowl.

He looked towards the chair propped under the door knob. He knew now why he had taken this precaution; he knew where his own fear lay, and it was not the fear of Broken Wagon with its posted sentries and its ear cocked for a war whoop. Carney, too, would have headed straight for Muleshoe and the rock beyond. And Carney would start smelling out the trail from there.

Damn, but he wanted to sleep, to be free of all this thinking. Like a squirrel in a cage, the way a man's mind scampered nowhere. Then he heard a stirring just beyond the door. Instantly he was alert and reaching for the gun he'd laid on the floor beside the bed. The door knob was being turned ever so slowly. He called out, "Who's there?"

Her voice was low. "Helen Addison, Neil."

He felt warmth strike through him, but greater than the warmth was reluctance. He couldn't have said why. Then he remembered Ben Hare's guess about what had driven Jud Addison to his drinking, but it wasn't Addison he pitied at this moment. He said, very gently, "No, Helen," and then he said again, "No," just as gently.

He heard the whisper of her feet as she moved away, and he turned over in the bed and tried willing himself to sleep.

CHAPTER EIGHT

Hill Road

When Bowman walked into the *Bugle* plant next morning, Jenny was sitting at the roll-top desk, a batch of galley proofs spread before her. Reading swiftly and making an occasional correction, she was so intent upon her task that she didn't look up when Bowman closed the door behind him.

Bowman stood watching her. In this unguarded moment her face was like a child's, sweet and unmarred by worry; she might have been playing at dolls. Then she became aware of him and turned and gave him a nod, and the illusion was gone. He crossed over, looked into the rear room, and saw Ben Hare busily setting type, his fingers flying from the founts before him to the stick he held in his hand. Ben Hare, too, was wrapped in his own deep concentration. Bowman said good-morning to him, and Hare glanced up and grinned.

125

"News, chief," the printer announced. "Events have transpired, and the world awaits them breathlessly."

"I know," Bowman said. "The camp is besieged by howling savages and we're all about to be massacred."

"Bigger than that, Neil. Ogden got his beef contract last night."

Bowman said, "Come in here, Ben. I want to talk to both of you."

Hare obediently put down his work, wiped his hands on his apron, and came slouching into the office.

Jenny shoved the proofs aside and swung the swivel chair about so that she faced Bowman. She said, "I take it you've decided on a policy for the paper." As she worked, she'd been running her free hand through her dark hair so that wisps stood in wild disarray. She pushed back her hair, and the gesture, so utterly feminine, pleased him. She was human enough to have her small vanities. Bowman smiled.

Hare said, "You have the floor, chief. Commence the oration."

Bowman shook his head. "First, I want to know all about this beef contract business."

Hare seated himself on the edge of the littered pine table; in the closeness of the office, the smell of whisky was strong on him. "The miners met at the Imperial last night," he said. "Object: to discuss what must be done about the Indian menace. With a scalp lifted right here in camp, the ant hill was kicked over for certain. Ogden favoured the assemblage with some oratory. He was calm, cool, and persuasive. He recommended a ring of sentries. And he worded the recommendation so well that everyone forgot that they'd already had the same idea and that some sentries were already posted. Then Ogden pointed out that as long as the flower of the camp — his expression, not mine — was assembled, it was an excellent time to settle the matter of meat for the winter. In short, he seized opportunity by the forelock."

Bowman asked, "When did he start being interested in the meat business?"

Jenny said, "The problem's been on everybody's mind this fall. Having a bad snowstorm so early has made the miners nervous. Broken Wagon is high enough to get blocked in if the winter should be anywhere nearly as bad as the last one. We could have starvation here. The Miners' Council called for bids a month ago. They offered to back anyone interested in starting a packing plant and butcher shop

127

by putting up half of the original investment. Kemp Satterlee, who runs Circle 6 ranch over in the Twosleep, made a bid."

Bowman nodded. "His foreman, Pete Beale, was on the stage the other night. I remember that Hascomb asked him about Satterlee's beef. Beale said his boss was holding what he had against the chance of getting the beef contract."

"Actually, Satterlee never stood a chance," Jenny said. "He's been suspected of rustling for years. His bid was suspiciously low. Nobody could supply beef at the price he named unless someone else was paying the cost of raising that beef. The miners realised that. Ogden's bid was higher, but even so, it was accepted last night."

"Did Ogden say where he'd get his beef?"

She shook her head. "Not exactly. Ben tells me he simply said he'd buy good grade beef wherever it was available in the ranching country. Nobody pressed the point."

Ben Hare spread his hands and grinned his wicked grin. "It's very simple. Satterlee will rustle beef from his neighbours, and Ogden will buy the beef from friend Satterlee at a low price, and both of them will make a profit. The camp hasn't seen that Ogden and Satterlee are closer than two crows in a corn patch."

"So Satterlee's part of the opposition," Bowman mused. "Faro was careful not to speak of Miles's fight against Ogden while Pete Beale was listening. Now I understand why. But what if a partnership between Ogden and Satterlee could be proved to the miners?"

"Ah," Hare said, "now you're thinking as Miles thought. He believed that if such a partnership could be brought to light, Ogden's cardboard throne might crumple so that he'd be driven from Broken Wagon. Every miner might turn against him, for every mucker in the diggings is also a partner in this venture. No man wishes to salt his food with the knowledge that he's been duped. What wrath is so righteous as when simple men are made fools?"

"One scrap of evidence, and the *Bugle* could throw a broadside at Sig Ogden," Jenny said. "As it is, all we can do is insinuate."

Bowman moved away from the stove. In him was a tingle of excitement, the feel of the hunter who sees his way to close in for the kill. He crossed to the desk and picked up the sheaf of proofs and shuffled through them. His eyes fell on a story about Bart Carney's escape from Deer Lodge. He would have liked to read that closely, but he passed it by. There was another story, obviously set up last night, about the man killed and scalped. Bowman shook his head. Then he found what he sought. Hare had been working on the beef contract story this morning, running off galley proofs as the type was set up. The account was as yet incomplete, but all the man's talent for deviousness showed in what he'd composed.

"Looks like you were going to give it the full front page," Bowman said.

Lines caught his eye here and there: "The *Bugle* questions how Mr. Ogden hopes to obtain honest beef and still show a profit for himself on this venture. . . . Did Mr. Satterlee's appearance in camp as recently as the day the contract was awarded indicate that a partnership was in the offing?"

Bowman looked up. "It won't do," he said.

He saw that Hare was studying him. The printer said, "Jenny provided the music, and I found the words. It's a work of collaboration. Let me depart from my first metaphor to say that it should sow a few seeds of doubt."

Bowman singled out the proofs pertaining to the beef-contract story, tore them across and walked to the pot-bellied stove. He thrust the torn papers inside, and the clang of the stove door as he shut it made a loud sound in the silence. "Pi the type on the whole account," he said. "I want a small item saying the contract was awarded. No more than that. Not one word of editorial comment."

He might as well have slapped them both. Hare stiffened, then took on a stern look. Like a deacon, Bowman thought. For all the world like a Hard-Shell Baptist deacon staring at sin and blasting it with his silent disapproval. Half a rogue, this man? Then Hare shrugged and the frost in his face melted under a smile that was wholly evil. Jenny stood up. Disappointment and anger tightened her mouth, and her voice shook. "You don't mean to fight Ogden?"

"I mean to fight him to a standstill," Bowman said. "But not this way."

Jenny said, "Miles worked for weeks on this. Weeks! His trip to Helena was part of his campaign. He wanted to hire a range detective to watch where Ogden bought his beef if he got the contract. Faro says that

131

Miles couldn't find the right man. Just the same, we can't drop what he started."

Bowman said, "There was a bargain set down in writing, remember. It says that I dictate policy here. That means we'll handle this my way."

Jenny said, "So already we stand opposed. Yesterday you wondered when that would happen."

He looked at her and tried to make his appeal without speaking. He wanted to ask for her trust, but his tongue was locked because of Ben Hare's presence. He couldn't say that he didn't trust Hare because Hare had proposed a bargain by which the spoils would be divided. He couldn't even think that, not when he wasn't sure whether Hare was really looking for the main chance or whether the man was being deviously loyal and putting him, Neil Bowman, to the test. He could only shrug. "That's the way it stands," he said.

Jenny said flatly, "Then I think Miles's biggest mistake was his last mistake."

Bowman turned and walked out of the place, feeling their eyes on his back. He began trudging the planking of Placer, turning over in his mind all that had just been said. He knew he had stood before those two people first as a stranger and at the last as an enemy, distrusted and beyond their understanding. But now he knew what his next step would be. He had finally learned what he'd hoped to learn from Faro in the stagecoach — the nature of the fight between Miles Hascomb and Sig Ogden and the means by which Hascomb had hoped to win that fight. Again he felt the excitement of the hunter closing in for the kill.

Around him Broken Wagon went about its business of the day. There were still a great many miners in the camp, held here by the Indian scare. He had meant to ask Ben Hare or Jenny the latest news that had come over the wire about the Sword-Bearer uprising, but he hadn't got to it. Warmer to-day, he noticed, and although the sky was still overcast, he judged that the sun might yet break through. The snow was melting and mud was everywhere. It squished under the loose planking, oozed up through cracks, and made the street a brown and treacherous sea.

Up on the south slope, carpenters were at work putting up a new building. It looked as though it would be a sizeable one. He had heard the beat of hammers and the rasp of saws while he breakfasted at the restaurant. He came abreast of the saloon where the Indians had squatted yesterday, but they were gone. A good thing, likely, with hysteria high. He reached the livery stable where he'd left his horse and went inside and saddled up the roan. The package of food he had got from the restaurant last evening had been left with his gear. Stale food now, but it would do. He tied the package to his saddle.

The hostler came in just as he was tightening the cinch, Bowman asked, "How do I get to Circle 6?"

"Follow the street on through the camp and climb the hump," the hostler said. He spat tobacco juice into one of the stalls. "From the top, you'll be looking down into the Twosleep. Ranching country, all of it. About five, six miles down the other side, you'll find a trail cutting off to the right. It's good for going down but hell for coming up. It will lead you to Kemp Satterlee's doorstep."

"Thanks," Bowman said.

"You aim to ride alone?"

"Why not?"

The hostler spat again. "Well, I suppose it ain't likely that Indians will be showing themselves by daylight. And there's always traffic over the hump. Things can't stop stock-still just because of a few pesky red-skins. That's what Sig Ogden told us last night. He meant it, too. At the crack of dawn he had carpenters at work."

Through the thin walls of the stable, Bowman could still hear the distant beat of hammers. "That new building on the slope?"

"It'll be our packing plant," the hostler said. "Quite a shebang when it's finished, I'll wager. Nothing to shade the layout that Frenchman, the Marquis de Mores, built over at Medora in Dakota four years ago. But mighty good for Broken Wagon."

"If I remember my newspaper reading," Bowman said, "the Frenchman went belly up sometime last year. So did a couple of Miles City buckos who'd built a plant."

"Sig will pull through," the hostler insisted. "Hell, ain't the whole camp behind him?"

"Time will tell," Bowman said.

He led the roan outside and mounted and rode along Placer, heading east. Last night he'd been too troubled to think how good it had felt to be back in a saddle again. He walked the horse through the mud. He saw Ben Hare cutting diagonally across the street and watched as the printer headed into the Imperial. Going for

135

a drink, Bowman supposed. He remembered what Hare had said about Ogden's whisky being good if you could lay hands on the right bottle.

He rode on. When he came abreast of the cross street that led up the slope to the Addison place, he saw Helen Addison descending the hill, picking her careful way, a market basket on her arm and a shawl pulled about her shoulders. He had not seen her this morning when he'd left the house. He lifted his hat to her and called a good morning across the distance, meaning to do no more than that. Then, on an impulse, he neck-reined the roan and headed up the slant towards her. He pulled to a halt and looked down at her and smiled.

"Hello," he said.

"Hello," she replied. She met his eyes frankly, yet he had the feeling that doing so cost her an effort of will. His own strong sense of embarrassment, he knew, must be echoed in her. She said, "I want you to know I'm ashamed of myself. About last night."

He shook his head. "I fell dead asleep right away. I don't know a thing about last night."

Her handsome face softened, and gratitude stood plain in her eyes. He didn't begrudge the lie, seeing what it did for her. She moved closer and lifted a hand to his saddle. She said very intently, "Any woman could grow lonely if she were left too long alone. There is just one thing I want you to know; I have never tapped on any other man's door."

Bowman said, "He'll come back. They tell me he always does."

"Yes," she said, "he'll come back. But never all the way. Never over the wall between us."

"And what kind of wall is that?"

"The wall of pride. The highest of them all."

"But that's only something he's built in his mind."

She shook her head. "You don't understand. He came from a dirt-poor family in Illinois. He went West when he was in his teens and he came back home with talk of a rich claim in Montana. He had the courage then to court the girl who lived in the biggest house on the highest hill. Our honeymoon was his return trip West. But the claim petered out. The night that he discovered he was poor again was the first night he came home drunk."

Bowman said, "But he must have struck

it rich later," and he waved his hand towards the house, remembering what he'd thought last night as he looked at the furnishings.

Again she shook her head. "We drifted, always lured by some tale of a rich strike somewhere farther on. Finally we came here, to another hovel in another boom camp. I couldn't face the prospect happily. But about that time my father died, and I came into a small legacy. I ordered the big house built. And I had the furniture from the farm in Illinois freighted out. I told Jud I'd grown tired of living like an animal and that with the legacy we didn't have to. I shouldn't have done any of it. I know that now. I spent everything I had on a home, the first one we'd ever owned. The house hit Jud hard. When the furniture came, he went on his worst drinking bout. And he ceased being a husband to me."

"No man can run from reality," he said. "He'll have to face that fact sooner or later."

"I spoke of a wall," she said. "It's real enough. Could you climb such a wall as the one I reared against Jud Addison? Could any man?"

"I don't know," he said. He tried to smile at her again and couldn't; her trouble

138

was too deep. In an instant he had glimpsed the mistake with which she lived, and it had been frightening to see. He had come up this slope to bring her comfort, remembering last night, but there was no comfort he could give her. He touched his hand to his hat brim and reined the roan about and rode back down to Placer.

Again he followed the street, and soon he was at the far fringe of the town where Placer Street became a road climbing into the hills. The road was a series of sharp switchbacks, brush-bordered and awash with the runoff of melted snow. At the first turn he found a man with a rifle stationed, one of the miner-sentries. The man nodded at him. The roan laboured on up-wards, and at another rise Bowman could look down upon the roofs of Broken Wagon and the treetops and across them to Cemetery Hill. Again a flat-bed wagon was up there, surrounded by a handful of people, and he wondered who was being buried this morning and then remembered the nameless bummer who had died in the dark. He shuddered, thinking that now he was seeing a funeral that might have been his own.

Here at this high place, the air was sharply clean and fragrant with pine. He sat his saddle longer than he realised before he jogged his mount onwards.

Clearly to him then came the strike of hoofs against rock on the road below. Someone riding along a lower switchback. It could be anyone; the muddy ruts of the road showed that fresh traffic had already gone over the hump this morning. He peered back over his shoulder, but the horseman was hidden from him by the trees and the looping road.

It could be anyone, he reminded himself again. Why then did Bart Carney stand out so strong in his thinking?

CHAPTER NINE

Tossed Coin

Made a difference to a man to have a horse under him, Bart Carney decided. A heap big difference. Made his shadow tall and gave him the feeling that he could show fast heels to anybody who might be hankering to catch up with him. Not that this Muleshoe mount he rode was anything to win blue ribbons. But he was a bigawd horse just the same, and better than none. Better than flatfooting it over a considerable hunk of Montana Territory with hay in his hair from the stacks he slept in and hunger in his gut, with outsize clothes flapping on him that he filched from clotheslines in the dark of the moon so as not to have that damn' prison garb showing. Jake Mapes, at Muleshoe, had fixed him up with some levi's and an old blanket coat and found a saddle to throw on the horse, though the saddle looked as if it might dissolve come a good rain.

Trouble was, Jake hadn't been any friendlier than the law allowed and had sort of shooed Bart Carney along as soon as breakfast was done with this morning.

Jake had changed, no fooling about that. Jake had been one of those ranchers Bart Carney could count on for a horse sound of wind and limb whenever a posse had been pressing him too hard in the old days. He'd done right by Jake, too, in those times, leaving sacks that jingled on Jake's doorstep. Jake had got his ranch paid for a lot quicker because of the money Bart Carney had given him, and Jake hadn't ached from any stricken conscience because it was stolen money. Jake had always had a big grin for him when he showed up to grab a meal and a change of mounts.

Well, it was some different now with Bart Carney fresh busted out of stony lonesome and the newspapers screaming his name and the telegraph wires humming with it. Jake had seemed jumpy from the moment Bart Carney had showed at Muleshoe last evening, and maybe he couldn't blame Jake. Jake was mortgage-free and pot-and-window prosperous now, and it wouldn't do to have bounty hunters cornering Bart Carney in Jake's parlour.

And the man had given him grub, duds, and money, a gun, a horse, and gear. It was as much as he, Carney, had hoped for.

Just the same, Jake had changed. But the whole country had changed, and not to Bart Carney's liking. Surprising what a difference six years could make. A heap more barbed wire than there'd been. Roads where once a man would have found nothing but game trails. Farmers taking the place of the man on horseback. Railroad trains raising a big stink. Damned if Montana wasn't turning into a tame chunk of territory. Still, Jake could have asked him to lay over a few days, what with this unseasonable snow on the hills and talk of the Indians being out. Not that Bart Carney would have lingered. He had an Indian of his own to look for, one carved out of rock by the freakish winds and rains of a thousand years.

Mighty cold to-day. Carney huddled deeper into the blanket coat. Better this cold than the warmth of Deer Lodge's tight-pressing walls. And better this road, snow-choked and snaking through a corridor of high-lifting pines than the narrowness of a cell. It made him young to be riding with the smell of pine in his nose, the mountain silence all around him, and the free sky overhead. He'd sleep well tonight, even though he'd be wrapped in a tattered blanket with nothing between him and the ground but some pine boughs.

"You sure as hell did a lot of tossing and turning," Jake had told him at breakfast. "Talked in your sleep, too. A bunch of crazy gibberish."

Well, when a man's nerves got tight, he was bound to squirm around and maybe sing out in his sleep. But when you were in a business where it paid to be tight mouthed, you didn't want to be gabbing when you didn't know about it. He wondered how much of a habit sleep talking had got to be. Neil Bowman had never mentioned it, but likely he spoiled Neil's sleep many a night when they shared a cell.

Where was Neil riding these days, and how did he fare? Wasn't so long ago they'd shaken hands just before Neil had gone through the gate with a pardon in his pocket. Neil would be some surprised to read in the papers that Bart Carney had walked out, too, practically on his heels. Damned if he hadn't liked Neil. The boy had stuff in him that made him different from most of the sour birds you found in a prison yard. Odd, though, that Neil hadn't quite been able to meet his eye when they

144

parted. He kept remembering that about Neil.

Likely he'd never see the boy again. Neil must have struck out for his Yellowstone Valley; and once Bart Carney did himself a little digging job, he was going to beeline to hell out of Montana. The Mexican border was the place to winter. A lot of miles lay between here and Sonora, and likely a lot of law men, too, but an old wolf still had his savvy. And a horse beneath him. Not much of a horse, but he'd buy him a better one when he laid hands on that loot.

Twenty thousand dollars, coin of the realm. Twenty thousand in good greenbacks waiting to be spent!

He kicked the horse to a trot but didn't hold to that pace long. The road climbed, and in some places the snow had drifted across so deep he had to dismount and lead the horse. He began to grow panicky, wondering if he could make it to the point which he must reach. Damned if he wanted to wait around these hills till a thaw came.

"Some wagons over the road," Jake had told him this morning when he asked. "Not many, though. A horse-backer went up there a couple of days ago. Stopped off for a meal on the way. A fellow in his mid-twenties, I'd say. Long-faced and big-boned. I didn't peg him for a law man, but there's no telling."

A hell of a description that had been! Could have fit a lot of fellows. Could have fit Neil Bowman, for instance, or a hundred others. Maybe that was what had got him, Bart Carney, to thinking about Neil this morning.

Noon was coming on. No sun showing to tell time by, but his gut hollered that it had been hours since breakfast. Jake had packed grub for him, but he was too near the rock now to want to waste time eating. Snow had buried a lot of landmarks, but he had the feeling in his bones that this was familiar country and not far from his destination. At each turn he was lifting his eyes and being disappointed. At each turn the hope surged again. Damn, but that stone Indian surely hadn't taken off to join up with that crazy Sword-Bearer Jake had talked about. He grinned at his own wild notion.

Imagine the Indians hitting the warpath in this year of the Lord 1887! It had almost been good news, hearing about it. Proved that the whole Territory hadn't turned to the plough and peace. Made it seem as though some small chunk of the old days was left. Bart Carney could remember when the redskins had lifted a few scalps along the stage road between Virginia City and Bannack. He'd been in his twenties then and riding with the Road Agents, though he hadn't cottoned to that bunch, being mostly a lone wolf. Those boys had found it mighty handy to lay trouble to the Indians. A few of the quick-triggered ones like Haze Lyons and Boone Helm and George Ives had walked free and unsuspected many a time because their killings could be blamed on the Bannacks. He shook his head, remembering. He never favoured unnecessary gunplay, and it had proved the wiser policy. Those Road Agents were dead now and planted deep in various boot-hills, their necks stretched long by Vigilante ropes.

A man put a lot of years behind him, and a lot of memories.

Another turn ahead, and he rounded it and lifted his eyes to the profile of the rock Indian above him, sharp etched against the sky. He had looked for this Indian all of the morning and then had been so deep in thought that he'd come upon it in complete surprise. He sat his saddle then and found himself strangely empty of feeling.

He discovered that his hands were shaking. He grinned his old wolf grin and forced himself to make up a cigarette and take time to light it, thus drawing out this moment and tasting its fullness.

Then he was down from his horse and wading through the snow. Running nearly. And fear struck through him, colder than the day. He didn't have to sight from the Indian to find the lightning-blasted pine, and he didn't have to do any measured pacing to see the discarded shovel near the raw earth, heaped black and dusted over by a light fall of snow. Even so, he didn't want to believe what his eyes told him. He ploughed onward until he could look into the emptiness of the hole. He fell to his knees and pawed into the hole as though his hands might find something his eyes told him wasn't there. He got to his feet. Nearby he found the empty Wells Fargo box in a clump of bushes.

After that he stood for a long time, the cigarette dead and forgotten between his lips, his mind numb and his body numb.

Finally, anger came, beating through him in hot waves, turning him murderous. That damn' horsebacker who stopped at Jake's! After the anger came calmness, and he was the old wolf again, wary and sharp-minded. He moved about, looking for sign. Horse tracks, sure enough, plain in the snow. He struggled back to his own horse, mounted, and began to follow the tracks.

Fresh, but not too fresh. Here were horse droppings a day or so old. Here the tracks stood out boldly and could be followed as fast as his horse could flounder, but there were open spots where the wind had got at the slope and drifted the snow. But the tracks were leading downhill, and by descending he always found them again. That long-faced gent hadn't wanted to take the road back past Muleshoe, not with the burden he'd been carrying. Carney harked up a map of the region in his mind. The man who'd beat him to his loot had cut straight down the slope toward the stage road that ran west to east from Helena to Whitewater Gulch.

Then he came upon the dead horse.

The sign was plain to read — the dead-fall unseen in darkness, the broken leg, the merciful bullet behind the animal's ear. No saddle. And now there were the tracks of a man to follow.

He came out upon the stage road in late afternoon. A wider road than the one up from Muleshoe. A road that bore a great deal more traffic. He looked up this road and down it; the road stood empty. Empty as his mind had been from shock when he'd found that gaping hole and put all his faculties to the job of trailing. But now he was thinking again, thinking clearly.

Who could have known how to go straight to the place where the money had been buried? Who could have read his mind? He remembered Jake Mape's telling him how he'd talked in his sleep last night. Was Jake the man? But Jake had been standing in the yard when Bart Carney rode off this morning. Jake couldn't have got up the slope ahead of him. The sign had been too old, and besides, that dead horse hadn't packed the Muleshoe brand.

No, Bart Carney had talked in his sleep another night. And there had been only one person who might have listened.

Again he looked both ways along the road. Helena in one direction, with its bright lights and many pleasures for a man loaded down with twenty thousand dollars. Whitewater Gulch in the other direction, and that new boom camp, Broken Wagon, which Jake Mapes had told him about. Bright lights or back country — which would have been Neil Bowman's choice?

For a long while Carney sat his saddle,

trying to think how it would have been for Neil Bowman, trying to make the right guess. No trailing the man on a road pocked by the passage of many. At last he fished into his pocket and found a small coin from the fund of money Jake had given him. He called the shot in his mind, sent the coin spinning, and caught it and slapped it on the back of his hand. Then he looked to see if it was heads or tails. . . .

Faro's room on the second floor of Broken Wagon's one hotel gave him a view of Placer, and from the window he had seen Neil Bowman go into the *Bugle* office this morning and later emerge to walk along the planking in the direction of the livery stable. Faro had watched morosely, his mood grey as the sky. He had arisen early, hours before his usual time, for his table at the Imperial held him until long after midnight. He had dressed with care, as always, and had his breakfast and returned to his room. Now he sat hating the room and the day and himself.

All the rooms had been the same in all the frontier places where he'd stopped; all the days had been the same, holding little sunshine for him. And his mirror this morning had showed him more than the

151

grey in his hair; it had showed him his own shame. He tried not to think about that.

He could, when he allowed himself, recall a genteel background. He had long ago closed his mind to such rememberings. The lost cause of the Confederacy had washed a lot of drifters such as he to the far frontiers. Soft hands were made for a soft life, but they were also suited for the turning of cards. Once he had supposed that such work was but for the moment; a man had to live. Some day he'd find employment worthy of his station. Dodge City, Abilene, Cheyenne, Miles City, Helena, Broken Wagon — what a parade of towns there had been! This morning he wondered in which of them he'd lost the last shred of ambition and settled to the timeless days, the taut nights.

He shrugged away these thoughts. He inched his chair nearer the window, looked again for Bowman, and saw the man far down the street, almost out of his range of vision. A good figure of a man, Bowman. A fine stride he had, and a proud way of holding his head. Queer how the frontier had fashioned its own aristocracy, a breed of men not born to the purple like the fine blades of the magnolia South but hewed out of rawhide and oak. Still, there was something about Bowman that troubled him. He could remember the man's long face by lamplight in the room where Miles Hascomb had died. The brittle hardness of Bowman made him a little frightening. Was Bowman another who'd somewhere lost sight of a star that once had guided him?

Pointless speculation! He shook his head, and his restlessness compelled him out of his chair. On impulse he donned his cloak and went from the room and down the stairs. Suddenly he saw himself as a man fleeing from the shame that had come upon him last night. On the planking he paused, brought up short by this realisation; then he headed for the *Bugle* office. He came into it to find Jenny working on proofs at the big desk. She looked up and smiled, but her smile was troubled. In his eyes she was a fair child and a forlorn one, and he was quickly responsive to her mood.

"Good-morning, Jenny," he said.

"Good-morning, Faro. You're up early."

He shrugged. "There are times when there is no comfort in sleeping."

"Then take a chair and stretch out your legs. I'll be free shortly."

But he continued to stand. Jenny bent

over her work again, her pencil scratching occasionally as she made a correction on one of the galleys. In the back room Ben Hare was working; Faro could hear the clicking of type as it fell into the stick. When Jenny laid aside a galley, Faro cleared his throat.

"There was a question I wanted to ask," he said. "The funeral was no place for it. Did Bowman pay you the promised money?"

"Why, yes," she said. "He dropped in here yesterday afternoon, after you left."

"And he was here again this morning. I saw him from my window."

She frowned, tightening her fingers around the pencil so that he thought she was going to break it. "He was here," she said. "Here to scrap hours of Ben's work and mine. Here to tell us that the next issue must say nothing against Ogden." She shook her head. "Faro, I don't know what to make of him."

"Ogden's afraid of him," Faro said. "If that's any comfort to you. Deathly afraid."

Her face livened with interest. "You know that for certain?"

"Ah, yes," he said, and all the shame of last night swept over him again. He knew now why he'd come here: perversely he had wanted to lay that shame naked. "There was a miners' meeting at the Imperial. You know that — I saw Ben there covering it for the paper. After the meeting, business slacked off; the Indian scare made men too edgy for the pleasures. I closed my table early. Ogden called me to his office then."

Jenny had been studying him. "Whatever for, it was a sorry session," she guessed. "It's written plain on you."

"Oh, but we were gentlemen together," he said bitterly. "He poured me liquor from his sideboard and presented me with a fine cigar and lighted it for me. But even so, it was plain who was master and who was servant. The thing on his mind soon came out. He had, he told me, sometimes questioned my friendship with Miles Hascomb. Considering that the *Bugle* was opposed to him, it scarcely seemed fitting that an employee of his — he tempered that by calling me a *valued* employee — should be overly intimate with the enemy."

"He dared to tell you where to choose your friends?"

Faro made a small shrug. "He hoped that the change in management here would mean that I would no longer frequent this place. It was skillfully put. I asked him point blank about Bowman then, and he admitted his fear of the man. He said that Miles was a crusader, though often a misinformed one. He claimed that he respected Miles. But Bowman strikes him as nothing but an opportunist. In short, a crook smells the taint in another crook."

Jenny shook her head. "To think he'd tell you how you must live your private life!"

"Now you know," he said. "My being here now is an act of rebellion." But saying this, he knew that her quick perception must have told her the full truth, that he had not been defiant last night. No act by cold morning could change that. The baring of his shame had scarcely lessened it. He'd been bold enough to reprimand Pete Beale in the stagecoach, and bold enough to remind Bowman that although Hascomb was dead, he, Faro, still stood guard. Why had he been less bold, facing Ogden? Had something died in him with the full realisation that Miles Hascomb was dead?

He said with belated anger, "Ogden! In Virginia he wouldn't have been good enough to groom our horses!"

Ben Hare came from the back room; he was wearing his leather apron, but he had pulled on his coat. He nodded at Faro and grinned at Jenny and went out the front door to head slantwise across the street. Through the window Faro watched the stoop-shouldered figure shamble along; he shook his head. Any man who drank before noon would forever be a mystery to him.

Jenny said, "Miles valued your friendship very much. I'm in your debt because of that. I was thinking this morning that I'd miss seeing so much of you, now that he's gone."

She was, he knew, giving him his chance to keep his peace with Ogden and still do so with a pretence of honour. He wanted to reach eagerly for this gift; he wanted, at the same time, to reject it. He shook his head. "As for the debt, it is the other way around," he said. He was stricken then by a full sense of his loss. "God!" he cried. "Day before yesterday I was riding in a stagecoach with him. Yesterday I stood at his grave. To-day it's an empty world."

"Why?" she asked softly. "Why did he mean so much to you?"

The answer came readily; he had glimpsed it when he'd asked himself where his boldness had fled. "Because he was the man I once was and ceased to be," he said. "He was the courage I used to have, the conscience I no longer hear, the gentle strength I squandered. Does that explain?"

"Yes," she said. "I think it does." Then her attention was caught by something beyond the window, and he followed her gaze to see Neil Bowman riding along Placer, heading towards the hump. Jenny was frowning, her lips firm. She said, like one talking to herself, "Is that the enemy? Is that the man the courage and the conscience and the strength must be pitted against?"

She stood up, shoving the galleys aside as she did so. "I know what I'm going to do," she said.

Again it was as though she'd spoken a thought aloud, heedless of his presence. Faro looked at her and saw her as he had never seen her before. How could she be frail with woman's frailness and yet so resolute, so great in stature? He didn't know, but suddenly it was no longer an empty world. And it would never be, not so long as the seed of Miles Hascomb lived.

CHAPTER TEN

The Indians Again

Near noon Bowman reached the top of the rise and rode across the flat summit of the hill standing between Broken Wagon and the Twosleep. It was cold here, so cold that the mud of the road had stiffened into tortured sculpture. Sagebrush grew sparsely, rustling to a brittle breeze, and a few stunted trees showed, looking forlorn in the snow patches. Bowman shivered. A feeling of loneliness and depression came over him. He stopped to give the horse a breather but didn't linger long. Mighty high here. At least six thousand feet altitude, he judged. Along the roadside sticks were thrust to give the measure of the snow when real winter came. These sticks, he noticed, were notched up to ten feet. The smell of snow was in the air, and the sun hadn't yet broken through the overcast. The camp he had so lately quitted seemed in remembrance to belong to another world.

He moved on. There was a mile of flatness, bare and desolate, peopled only by the wind; and then the road began to dip downwards. He could look into draws filled with snow, and he saw a frozen creek. Then the road came around a shoulder of the hill, and a valley lay spread before him, coming to his view so suddenly as to take his breath away. Below lay an immensity of land bulwarked by a far wall of mountains, a majestic pile, snow capped, blue, and beautiful. Lesser hills tumbled at the foot of the mountains, and in the valley trees showed and the glint of free-flowing water and the lifting smoke of ranch houses.

This was the Twosleep. Cattle country. This was the kind of land to which he'd been born, not as big and sweeping as the Yellowstone country, perhaps, but familiar for all that. Good grazing down there, water, and wood. He felt like a man come home.

He was pulled now between two urges, the one to sit his saddle, drinking in the view, the other to be on along the road and thus dropping down into the valley. He jogged the mount again. He was hungry, he realised, but possessed of too great a sense of excitement to want to take time to eat. The road looped downwards in wide easy swings, with none of the sharp switchbacks of the west slope. Sometimes the curves swung inwards and sight of the valley was lost to him; at such times he was sheltered from the wind that prowled this height of land. Again, the curves swung out, following the shoulder of the hill, and he could see the immensity of the Twosleep. Once he was impelled to look backwards and upwards, and just for an instant he glimpsed a rider on the road. The moment was too short, the distance too great for him to identify the rider. He remembered the sound of hoofs against rock on the west slope and was at once alert.

He'd shaken Bart Carney out of his mind miles back. Carney wouldn't be closing in on him so soon. Carney would come, yes, but the old wolf would need time to scent out the trail. But there was Ogden to think about. Last night he'd decided that Ogden was too wise to order the lightning to strike twice, but this was another day and another place. A dead man could be dumped into one of the draws and not found till spring; and if his scalp was lifted, it would be one more death chalked up to the Indians. He unbuttoned his sheepskin to give himself quick access to his gun.

That rider must be a good mile behind him. And now the road had brought him far enough down the slope so that he was looking for the turnoff to Circle 6. He found the trail at about where the hostler had told him it would be, and he struck down it. Soon he was into timber, a stand of fir and pine, and he felt easier in his mind with this shelter around him. He realised then how the presence of that rider on the backtrail had nagged at him. He stopped here in the timber. He'd put the roan to a lot of work this last couple of hours, and in spite of the cold the climb had sweated the animal. He got down and wiped off the roan with a handful of pine needles. When he mounted again, he took a branching trail.

Warmer down here, and he was leaving sign in the pliable earth. Sure sign, if that rider was following him. He told himself, as he had on the far slope, that it was probably just some wayfarer bent on business across the hump. He closed all but a small part of his mind to that rider. He had other things to think about. He'd come into the Twosleep with no plan but to scout Circle 6; he'd got this notion from the account of Miles Hascomb's intention to hire a range detective to do this very job. Thus he'd turned off the trail that would have led him to Kemp Satterlee's door. Whatever he hoped to find, it would likely be here in the back country.

He knew and accepted the enormity of his task. He had made this acceptance before he'd left Broken Wagon. A heap of wilderness back in here, and he might ride for days and find nothing to fit into the hand he hoped to play. But there could always be luck. He burrowed deeper into what appeared to be a lesser valley, an offshoot of the mighty Twosleep, fingering into the hills at the foot of the slope. Timber here, but long stretches of openness, too. Snow patches, where the sun seldom reached, but grass showed in places, brown with autumn's brownness. Flowers grew in profusion here in the spring, he supposed, violets and evening primroses and a host of others. He passed a small cabin, its door and windows gone, its roof sway-backed and nearly fallen in. He'd seen such cabins in the Yellowstone, too, abandoned and forlorn, and wondered what tales they might have told.

All his thinking had tended backward since he'd looked upon the Twosleep.

Again the old days came crowding up, not the prison days that had plagued him last night, but the earlier, boyhood days. He'd got his measure of values in those days, and the early standards were hard to shake.

He had tussled with himself when he first looked upon Carney's buried loot. He'd known a strong temptation to take the money to Helena and turn it over to the law. He'd had to think of Sherm Wheeler then and what he had lost to Wheeler. But when he had steeled himself against so crazy a notion as giving up the money, the tussle hadn't ended. Not by a long shot. The hell of it was that even though the money had now gone into Ogden's hands, the fight still went on within Neil Bowman. Here on a trail spotted by cattle droppings, he listened to the creak of his saddle leather and questioned anew the choice he had made.

This thinking was swept out of him by the jingle of a bit chain not his own.

No more than the ghost of a sound, it might have been conjured out of imagination. He got out his gun. He'd been following an old cattle trail; now he pulled off it into the timber and came quietly out of his saddle and clamped a hand over the

164

roan's nostrils. He stood listening intently. The jingle of metal came to him again, clearly this time. No illusion, that; a horse was coming along the trail. He waited for horse and rider to loom up; he waited with the gun tight in his fist, and then the rider was abreast of him, and he expelled his breath in a great gust and stepped out from his concealment.

"Hello," he said.

Jenny Hascomb had changed her garb for a divided riding skirt, plaid shirt, and blanket coat since last he'd seen her. Her horse, a grey gelding, was a good one. He was astonished that she'd been so close behind him, for he was sure he had seen her through the *Bugle*'s windows as he'd ridden out of town. Then he remembered that he'd tarried to talk to Helen Addison.

He said, "So you've been following me."

She nodded. She'd had a moment of frightened surprise at sight of him, but already she had recovered; he could see that. She said, "Ever since you left camp."

"Why?"

"To see what you were up to."

"You don't trust me, is that it?"

"That's it," she said.

He'd learned to expect frankness from her; he had grown used to her forthrightness that seemed so oddly masculine in one so feminine. What surprised him was her smile. "You left sign a blind man could have followed," she said.

"And you sky-lined yourself up on the slope." He smiled, too. "Maybe we both need lessons."

"What brought you over here?"

Now he could have spoken up as he hadn't dared to do in Ben Hare's presence. But could he condemn Hare on the flimsy evidence against the man? He didn't know. This girl had suffered a loss with Miles Hascomb's passing, and she'd stood up well under that loss — too well, he reflected — but Ben Hare might be a last prop to her for all that. He shrugged. "The bear went over the mountain to see what he could see, Jenny. I did the same thing. Are you hungry?"

"I could eat," she admitted.

"I've got bread and cold meat. It would taste better beside a fire. Shall we risk one?"

"Why not? This is a civilised country."

"When a man gets scalped in the midst of four thousand people?"

"We talked about that last night, remember. I've thought about it since. I keep recalling that the man was wearing your coat. It was you they were after, and you alone."

"Just the same, there are Indians out roaming around," he said. But he began gathering wood for a small fire. Jenny dismounted and helped him. He got a tiny blaze going, building it close enough to a deadfall log to provide a seat for her. He unwrapped the package of food, and they ate. In his prison days he had got so that he smoked rarely, but now he fished out a sack of tobacco and made up a cigarette. She reached for the makings and spun up one, too, accepting the brand he plucked from the fire.

"You smoke often?" he asked.

"Not very," she said. "It's something Miles taught me when I was in my midteens. When we were hungry, tobacco kept us from thinking too much about it."

"You were often hungry?"

She had taken no more than two or three drags from her cigarette. Now she tossed it into the fire and sat with her chin cupped in her hands, the heat of the fire flushing her cheeks, her eyes, so big and sombre, intent with thinking. Wisps of her black hair showed under the wide-brimmed hat she wore; she looked tomboyish, but altogether lovely.

167

She shrugged. "No point in talking about hunger," she said. "There is never any point in looking backwards. Besides, it isn't hunger I remember most but the running, the constant looking for a new place to light. At each camp, each cow town, I'd ask myself if this was where home was going to be. It never was."

He thought of Helen Addison and of how she, too, had followed a man who followed the will-o'-the-wisp. But it was not the same thing.

He stood up. "I'm for moving along." He began stomping out the fire. She stood up, too, and stretched herself, a gesture more carefree than any other he'd yet seen her make. Suddenly he felt very close to her; they had shared a fire, food, and tobacco, and for an instant they were no longer strangers. Then he remembered that she had followed him because she did not trust him.

"I want to see if Satterlee has got anything poked away back here," he said. "Some cattle with the wrong brands would be interesting. Especially if they were being butchered for the new packing plant that Ogden is building."

Her face livened. "Do you think there might be — ?"

"I don't know," he said. "But if the *Bugle* is to hit Ogden, I want it to be with something solid. The miners are for him because they're his partners in the packing plant deal. Talk to the hostler in Broken Wagon if you want to learn how the camp feels. If the paper only insinuates, we'll just get antagonism in return. Speak softly now and we'll make that much more thunder when we get something to roar about."

She turned thoughtful. "I think," she said at last, "that I owe you an apology."

He shook his head. "I've told you only half my plan. You may not like the rest of it."

There had been food to spare. He packaged what remained and tied it to his saddle. They mounted and in openness rode stirrup to stirrup; but where the trail ran through timber, Bowman took the lead. They kept the horses at a walk; they were cruising aimlessly, but when they came upon a creek and Bowman would have splashed across it, Jenny said, "This is Sheep Creek. Let's follow along it. If there's any activity back in here, it will probably be close to water."

"You know this country?" he asked, surprised.

"A little," she said. "I've ridden it before.

With Miles. When Satterlee first made his bid for the beef contract, we got your same notion of scouting Circle 6."

"Any sort of building back in here?"

"The old Hackett place. We're really on the border line of Circle 6 now. The Hacketts were people who trailed cattle from Oregon in the sixties. The family finally died out. This is public domain, but Satterlee uses it sometimes for summer graze."

"I'd like to see the Hackett place," he said.

"We can't be more than a mile or so from it."

She now took the lead, following the meanderings of Sheep Creek. Willows fringed the creek, and black birch and quaking aspen. Silence dwelt back here, and loneliness; sometimes an eagle wheeled far overhead, but there was no bark of squirrels, no scolding of jays. The sun was breaking through the overcast, but often they were under a canopy of boughs and thus still in a darkened land. After a while they came out upon a clearing where a house stood.

It was a two-story house made of logs from which most of the chinking had fallen, but still the place looked substantial. Barn, outhouse, and corral were also in fair shape. But for the glassless windows of the house, over which someone had hung burlap sacking, and the absence of smoke from the mud-plastered rock chimney, the place might have been a habitation. On impulse Bowman halloed as they entered the clearing, but there was no answer. Still, the yard was crisscrossed by many hoof marks; riders had been here, recently. From Circle 6, he supposed. He rode on to the barn and dismounted.

"I'd like a look around," he said. "We might as well put the horses under a roof."

They left both mounts in the empty barn. Crossing back to the house, Bowman shoved the door inward. They came into a kitchen that still held a rusty stove and a table. A box of kindling stood near the stove. Fresh kindling.

"Somebody's been here," Bowman murmured.

"Circle 6 has used this place for a line camp at times," Jenny said. "Maybe they're using it again."

Bowman nodded. The place seemed colder than the outdoors had been. He shivered involuntarily as he had on the summit. Both stepped from the kitchen into what had apparently been a combination dining-room and parlour, a big room echoing with emptiness. Nearly all the furniture was gone, used up for fire wood likely; and cows had got in here at one time and another. A door from this room led out of the house. Debris littered the corners — empty tin cans, old magazines, and what had once been a sewing machine. Bowman stood in the middle of the room looking about; Jenny prowled here and there.

"A saddlebag," she said from one of the corners and lifted up the object. "Empty," she announced, peering inside.

"Yes," he said and could have added another word: *Mine*.

He came and took the saddlebag from her and turned it over in his hands, excitement stirring him. No mistake about this being his. He frowned, wondering for an instant if he had been mistaken in charging Ogden with thievery. Had some drifting prospector or grub-line rider forced his way into the Addison place, found money to steal, and perhaps camped here last night? Or was the presence of the saddle-bags in a place sometimes used by Circle 6 merely proof that Satterlee and Ogden worked as one? He didn't know.

Then alarm touched him. He'd been

intent upon the saddlebag but not so intent as to miss hearing the approach of riders. They were out there in the yard, several of them from the sound; he glided swiftly to one of the windows and lifted the burlap sacking aside. Jenny had heard, too; she crowded close beside him. He let the sacking fall and turned and grasped her tightly by the arm.

"Indians," he said. "About half a dozen of them."

He saw fear rise in her, the same fear that had held the passengers of the stagecoach and last night gripped the camp, and he supposed such a fear was mirrored in his own face. He said quickly, "There's a white man with them. Pete Beale, Satterlee's foreman. That doesn't mean we're safe. I'm beginning to understand a lot now."

"What shall we do?" she whispered.

"I'm going outside," he said. "I'll try to make them believe I'm alone. If I can get them away from here, you come out then. And cut for camp."

He saw the protest in her eyes; he saw her lips move. He shook her roughly. "Do as I say!" he insisted. "It's the only chance."

CHAPTER ELEVEN

Death Warrant

When he stepped out of the house, he pulled the parlour door shut behind him, put a shoulder to the door frame and leaned indolently, hoping his high excitement did not show. From the window he'd recognised Beale by the man's buffalo coat, the Indians by their coppery faces. With the knot of riders drawing closer to the house, he saw that the Indians wore mocassins and two or three of them had feathers stuck in their hatbands and wore the high crowns of those hats undented; otherwise their garb was that of working cow hands. Very little buckskin and no cartwheel war bonnets. Some, though, wore blankets over their shoulders. The six, Bowman decided, were the same Indians he'd seen squatting before a saloon in Broken Wagon.

In his mind he willed Jenny to stay hidden; he had not dared look back at her as he left the room.

He grinned at Beale and lifted his hand in a lazy salute.

"Hello, Pete," he said.

Beale had already recognised him; surprise showed on the foreman's blocky face. "What the hell are you doing here?" Beale demanded.

Edgy! Bowman thought. Too edgy. "Taking a ride to look at the country," he said. "Lost my horse."

Beale reined up, and the Indians did likewise. "If you ask me," Beale said, "you're hell on horses, mister."

"This one I didn't have to shoot, Pete. It was a livery stable mount. I got off him a mile back, and he bolted. A roan. You didn't happen to see him?"

Beale shook his head. "Nary sign."

Bowman walked out from the doorway and came up to the shoulder of Beale's horse. The Indians regarded him unblinkingly. "Give me a hand up, Pete," Bowman said, "I'm damned tired of walking."

This was the moment when the explosion could come, he knew. He had played his game of bluff, wanting to keep Beale and his crew out of both the house and the barn, but Beale had not been pleased to find him here, and Beale must either show his true attitude now or counter bluff with bluff: Bowman could imagine the workings of that dull mind; he could see the indecision on Beale's face. What in hell was the new part owner of the *Bugle* snooping hereabouts for? Was this Bowman up to something, or was he telling it straight about losing a horse? Beale, Bowman decided, would be a mighty angry man if he ever found himself duped. The slow-thinking minds worked that way.

Beale scowled down at him. Then Beale freed his boot from his left stirrup and extended his hand. "I'll take you to Circle 6," he said. "You can get a horse there."

Bowman swung up. He glanced at one of the parlour windows and thought he saw the burlap sacking move slightly. Frantically, silently, he implored Jenny to be careful.

Beale reined his mount about and walked it away from the Hackett place, and the Indians bunched behind. One of them spoke to another, but the words were in their own tongue, unintelligible to Bowman. Blackfeet, he wondered? Cree, more likely. Fugitives from Canada since the Riel Rebellion two years earlier.

Bowman said in Beale's ear, "For a man who was so jumpy about Indians the other night, you've picked queer company, Pete."

"These boys work for us," Beale said. "They're good boys."

"Wouldn't hurt a fly, I'll bet," Bowman said.

Beale merely grunted.

They were beyond the Hackett clearing and into timber. When they emerged into another open stretch, Beale broke his burdened horse into a gallop. Bowman tightened his arms around Beale's thick waist and felt the bulk of Beale's holster and gun beneath the buffalo coat. His own gun swung at his hip, but he was a prisoner for all that. The thought struck him that he might get at his own gun or Beale's and put it at Beale's back and so command the situation. He decided against such a move. He'd come here to scout Circle 6, hadn't he? And Beale was taking him right to the ranch. Moreover, the time wasn't ripe to make a play. He wanted this crew farther away from Hackett's so that Jenny might have her chance.

They were riding to the southeast, more south than east; and often they were in deep timber, but sometimes they were again in openness, and Bowman could look to the high lift of the far mountains.

To-day the Twosleep was a land of great distances and great silences lying vast beneath a sickly sun. After an hour or so, they came upon Circle 6 headquarters. The buildings sat upon a flat which was walled on three sides by timber and open only to the north — the usual low log ranch house of the mountain country, a barn, a bunkhouse, a cookshack, and peeled-pole corrals. The ranch house had a gallery fronting it and thus was more pretentious than most. The man who stood on the gallery as they came riding up was an ox of a man, big and blocky as Beale but far craftier of face. Frowning, the fellow watched as the Indians whirled on to the corrals and dismounted while Beale pulled up at the steps leading to the gallery.

"This is Neil Bowman, Kemp," Beale reported. "Says he lost his horse. I found him at Hackett's place." He put his emphasis on that last.

Bowman slipped to the ground. "You'd be Kemp Satterlee," he said. "I'll be obliged for the loan of a horse to get me back to camp. I can have a livery stable man ride him back to you to-morrow."

Satterlee had a toothpick in one corner of his mouth. Still frowning, he worked the toothpick across his mouth as he stood thinking. A man with a tremendous driving force to him, Bowman decided. A man like Sherm Wheeler, but not quite so arrogant, because Kemp Satterlee was not quite sure of himself. But the makings were there. The difference was that Satterlee, not yet throwing his full shadow, tempered ruthlessness with wiliness. Now he was making up his mind about the man who stood before him. Awaiting the decision, Bowman was glad for the gun he still carried. Also, he was aware of Beale still up on the horse. Bowman stepped a pace away from the horse and turned slightly so that a movement of his head would bring Beale into his range of vision. Then he stood cool and ready. But suddenly the man on the gallery smiled a large, expansive smile.

"Come in," Satterlee urged. "Hell, you can have the pick of my saddle string, but you'll need to rest a while, man. It's a few hours' riding from here to Broken Wagon. Come in, I say."

Bowman shrugged. He would play this Satterlee's way because there was no better way to play it. He walked heavily up the steps. He'd done a lot of riding to-day, after too many years out of the saddle, and he reckoned he'd be stiff as a plank from it.

Satterlee pushed open a door and motioned to Bowman to step inside. "I'll be right with you," Satterlee said. "Want to talk to Pete about a job of work."

Bowman walked into a room that held a few pieces of furniture, most of them homemade. On a table were some stockmen's journals and a saddler's catalogue from Cheyenne. A Franklin stove threw out warmth, but the room itself gave none; its bareness testified that Circle 6 was a bachelor's layout.

From a window overlooking the yard Bowman saw that Satterlee had walked out to Beale, who'd dismounted, and the two were standing close together talking. Beale was gesticulating towards the northwest. Bowman smiled. The problem that had been Beale's at Hackett's place was now being presented to Satterlee. Had they a spy on their hands? Or was this Neil Bowman as innocent as he pretended? But Bowman had his own questions to worry him. There had been nothing at Hackett's to excite him but that saddlebag. Was there something that lay beyond Hackett's, something that those two were now afraid he'd seen? And did the presence of those

Indians on Circle 6 spell what Bowman had suspected at first sight of them with Beale?

Presently he saw Beale mount again, rein his horse about, and start off at a fast lope. Almost due north.

Satterlee came into the house. He smiled at Bowman and was the hearty host, but the smile lay too fixedly upon his lips.

"About that horse —" Bowman began.

Satterlee waved a hand. "Getting near supper time. Hell, you think I want you to go back to Broken Wagon and tell folks that Circle 6 didn't even feed you? You'd best stay and put your feet under the table."

Again Bowman shrugged. He could get out his gun and thrust it into the big belly of Kemp Satterlee, but again he decided against any such play. His being here was getting to be a game of meeting what would come. Satterlee was no surer about him than Beale had been, and so Satterlee had chosen to hold him here awhile. But for how long? To give Pete Beale time to scout the vicinity for a stray livery stable roan? That, Bowman thought, was as good a guess as any.

"I could use some supper," he said.

"Make yourself at home," Satterlee

urged. "I want to talk to those lazy damn' Indians. The rest of my crew should be showing up any time."

Left to himself, Bowman watched from the windows. Where was Jenny riding now, he wondered? He made a measure of time elapsed and the distance to be covered and judged that she might have reached the summit above Broken Wagon. It was growing dusky; the sun had dropped behind the western hills, and a grey world awaited the night with ancient patience. Riders loomed up out of the timber and came across the clearing towards the buildings. Riding out of the northwest, he noticed. About eight of them. They passed beyond his view, and shortly he heard the clang of a hammer against an iron triangle, and he left the house and walked around it towards the cookshack, which was also the mess hall.

He found Satterlee coming to meet him, the host again. Bowman moved in file with the men to the wash basin by the mess hall door. Taking his turn, he then went inside and stood until Satterlee indicated a place for him to the right of the head of the long table. Satterlee's white crew sat down, a blank-faced, sunburned bunch. The Indians ate here, too, but they took places at the end of the table, apart from the others. Satterlee sat at the head. The cook, a gruff old man, brought in platters of steaks and these were passed from hand to hand. No man spoke more than was necessary during the meal. At its finish, Bowman got out his makings and built himself a cigarette. He offered tobacco and papers to Satterlee.

"I use these," Satterlee said and took a cigar from his pocket. He didn't light the cigar, he merely chewed on it.

Bowman said then, very deliberately, "If you'll pick out a horse for me —"

Satterlee shook his head. "You'll stay till morning," he said. "One of my boys just came down off the hump. It's snowing hard up there. You try that road to-night and you could end up coyote bait. Isn't that right, Moran?"

A man down the table looked up, caught unaware. "Yeah. Sure," he blurted.

The cook had got an overhanging lamp lighted, and in its glow Satterlee's jaw looked hard and his eyes looked hard, though his mouth was faintly smiling. Bowman glanced towards one of the windows. No rain silvering it, and if there was snow at the summit there would likely be rain down here, though a man could ride through several layers of weather in a few miles in the Montana mountain country. Still, there'd been sharpness in Satterlee's voice, as though the man, in his own mind, were done with pretence.

Bowman shoved back his chair and stood up. No one seemed to be paying him particular heed, least of all the stony-faced Indians, yet he felt that every man in the room was watching him carefully. "Okay," he said. "Where do I bunk?"

Satterlee went with him to the bunk-house, but three or four of the others trailed along, too. They kept their distance and were indifferent to Bowman — too indifferent. Inside, someone got a lamp lighted, and Satterlee said, "Take your pick of any of the empties." Bowman seated himself on the edge of a bunk and tugged off his boots. The rest of the white riders drifted in, and Satterlee left. Bowman judged that the man slept in his ranch house. The Indians didn't appear, and Bowman asked about them and learned that they slept in the barn.

There was a table here, with cards strewn upon it, and Bowman supposed there might be a nightly poker game, but the riders were apparently too tired for that. They began to strip down to their underwear and crawl beneath the blankets. Bowman crossed the room in his stockinged feet and stepped out of the place into a thick, moonless dark. At once a man loomed behind him.

"Where do you think you're going?" the man demanded.

"Answer a call, damn it!" Bowman said, but still the man stood there.

When Bowman came inside, he undressed. Very carefully he hung his gun belt on a peg near the bunk. He thought of slipping the gun under his pillow but changed his mind. He'd had his several chances to use that gun, but those chances were gone. Use it now, or show too intent an interest in it, and he would only be openly admitting his growing alarm. There were too many of them keeping guard over him. There were a hundred and one unknown hazards between him and the saddled horse he'd need if he were to escape this place. He might as well get his sleep.

Someone blew out the lamp. Grass-filled ticks whispered to the weight of bodies, and darkness held the room. Tiredness gathered him up and bore him away into a greater darkness. . . .

When he felt a hand upon his shoulder, he came out of sleep sluggishly. Someone was saying, "Come up to the house," and though the voice was familiar it took him a moment to remember Satterlee and so recognise his own whereabouts. The first grey of dawn was in the bunkhouse. By that faint light he made out Satterlee's face, blank as any Indian's. No genial host to-day, this man. Bowman climbed out of the bunk and began to get into his clothes. When he reached for his gun belt and swung it around his middle, he felt its lightened weight.

"My gun," he said in an even voice. "It's gone."

"Those thieving Indians," Satterlee said with a scowl. "Never mind, I'll get you another."

Like a damn' cat with a mouse! Bowman thought.

He was now fully awake. His sense of alarm had become so strong that it was no longer alarm but something else — something compounded of wariness and curiosity and a feeling that a long wait had ended. From that last he had almost a sense of relief. He followed Satterlee from the bunkhouse. Objects loomed vaguely in the yard, and lamplight glowed in the front windows of the ranch house. Two horses stood tethered to the gallery railing, and one of these he recognised as Pete Beale's.

When he entered the house a step ahead of Satterlee, he was prepared to find Beale in the room. It was Faro's presence that astonished him.

Satterlee closed the door and put his back to it, and he said in a hard voice, "All right, Bowman. We've had our fun, but the frolic's over. Just what the hell were you looking for when you came snooping on to my land yesterday?"

Bowman looked at Faro. The gambler's face was grey with weariness, and Faro's eyes were both puzzled and a little frightened. Beale merely looked sullen. As always, the strong smell of horses was on Beale, and Bowman now understood where Beale had ridden last night. His bad mistake, damn it, had been in not guessing sooner where Beale had gone — and why.

He said, "So you had to send to Ogden for orders, eh, Satterlee? You couldn't make up your mind about me till he did your thinking for you."

Satterlee said, "Damn you, the point is you were snooping!"

"No," Bowman said. "The point is that Ogden could see farther than you, so he sent Beale back to you with my death warrant. Don't shake your head, man. You're

187

trying to work up enough anger right now to make murder easy for you. Because that's what Ogden wants. You were just worried for fear I'd found something at Hackett's or beyond there that I shouldn't have found. Ogden would see the thing in a different light. To him it would be clear that you'd got me where you wanted me, where I need never be a nuisance again. Isn't that it?"

Satterlee lifted his shoulders and let them fall; his eyes squinted and laughter lay deep in them. "That's it," he said and stood completely done with pretence at last.

Faro made a feeble gesture with one hand. "First, hear me out," he said, and the appeal was to Bowman. "Beale came into the Imperial late last night, about quitting time. He talked with Sig. Later Sig called me to his office. He said he wanted me to ride back to Circle 6 with Beale. He muttered something about Satterlee having word he'd send back with me." Faro rose shakenly from his chair. "Don't you see? It was a typical piece of Sig's scheming. Night before last he told me I must choose between him and his enemies. Yesterday I defied him by walking into the *Bugle* office. Now he's making sure I'll belong to him.

He's tricked me into being a part of these doings."

Satterlee said, "You've guessed right, too, gambler. The note Sig sent by Pete is plain about you. You're to be in on the killing."

This is it! Bowman thought; yet in him was a queer sense of detachment, as though he watched all this with a spectator's impersonal curiosity. He thought of his gun and all the chances there'd been yesterday, and he knew that he'd waited too long.

He looked at Faro's suffering face. "You've still got a choice, Faro," he said. "How do you choose?"

But it was Satterlee who spoke up. "We're all walking out of here," he said. He came across the room to the lamp and blew out the flame that had turned pale in the morning light. "We're going for a ride, the four of us. A short ride into the timber. Faro is a smart man. He'll choose to ride back."

He looked at Bowman and inclined his head towards the door. "Let's go."

CHAPTER TWELVE

Full Circle

Bowman walked out of the house first, Satterlee right behind him. Faro came next, with Pete Beale trailing the gambler. This, Bowman thought, would be the way a man got marched to the gallows. He still couldn't find reality in the situation; he might have been walking through a nightmare. He only knew that he wasn't going to die without making a fight. His body felt stiff and unwieldy; he remembered that he'd expected this after yesterday's riding. He wondered how faithfully his muscles would respond if he spun about and threw a fist at Satterlee's jaw and then made a run for the distant timber. Not much chance, he figured. Another corner of his mind dwelt on Faro. Faro still hadn't indicated his choice. How much could he count on Faro?

At the foot of the steps, Satterlee said, "Pete, go and saddle up a horse for me and one for Bowman."

Beale said in a strained voice, "I ain't sure I like this, Kemp. Do we want the law on us? A man turns up missing, somebody's bound to get curious."

Bowman stirred with interest. Beale was saying only half of what was on his mind; Beale didn't cater to murder. Yet the very fact that Beale hadn't voiced his whole reluctance meant that the man belonged to Satterlee. No hope there.

Satterlee said savagely, "You fool! I'm making sure he won't be found close to the house. Now get those horses."

Bowman heard Faro draw in a gusty breath and expel it, heard him say the one word, "*Jenny!*"

That was when a full sense of reality hit Bowman, and horror washed through him, tightening the muscles of his stomach. In the grey of morning she was riding out of the timber from the west and crossing the clearing towards the ranch house. Behind her trailed Bowman's led livery stable roan. Bowman wanted to shout to her to turn back, to warn her that death dwelt here. The words crammed his throat, but he checked them, knowing again that he was too late.

She rode straight towards them and

pulled up in the yard and smiled down. "So you're safe," she said, looking at Bowman.

The irony of this was almost too much for him. He wanted to laugh and didn't dare lest his laughter sound wild. He managed to say, "I didn't expect to see you."

"Your horse strayed back to the livery stable last night," she said. "I began worrying when I heard about that. You'd said you were going to ride over towards Circle 6. I couldn't sleep anyway, so I decided to come looking for you."

He remembered a judgment Ben Hare had once made of him. "I'd hate to play poker with you!" Hare had said. Poker! He looked up at Jenny, knowing how much of what she'd said was a lie, and her face was impassive, almost serene. But still the horror was in him. He stepped to one side to get a look at Satterlee. The man's broad face had gone blank, but his eyes showed how deeply he was disturbed.

Bowman let himself laugh then. "Couldn't have been snowing too hard up on the hump, Kemp."

"No snow at all," Jenny said. "It was a nice night for riding."

Satterlee said, "Girl, haven't you heard that the Indians are out?"

192

Jenny shrugged. "Word came over the wire last evening that the soldiers have Sword-Bearer's bunch surrounded near Fort Meade. There'll probably be a small skirmish before it's finished. But the Indians have lost their taste for the war-path."

"No more scalped dead men, Kemp," Bowman said pointedly. "And a dead woman would turn the whole countryside into a kicked ant hill."

This was a moment more delicately poised than when he'd run his bluff on Pete Beale at Hackett's place. And just as he'd imagined the workings of Beale's mind yesterday, so he could almost see the thoughts of Kemp Satterlee now. Jenny's showing up here meant there would have to be two dead out in the trees, not one. And with consequences a hundred times greater than if only a newcomer like Neil Bowman turned up missing. Moreover, there was Faro for Satterlee to consider. The gambler merely stood, his face troubled but stern, his legs planted apart, his arms rigid. Faro might not have had the courage to save a Neil Bowman, but Jenny was another matter.

And Jenny smiled again. "Let's be starting back," she said. "The miners tried to discourage me from riding last night. They said I'd be hunting a needle in a haystack, combing this country by dark. They promised to put a search party out this morning. We'll probably meet them on the hill road. I want to see their faces when I show up with you."

"Sure," Bowman said. He walked to the roan and climbed stiffly to the saddle.

Faro said, "I might as well ride back with you," and moved to the horse that stood beside Beale's.

Beale stood watching Satterlee, as though waiting his cue. Satterlee's scowl suddenly broke, and he smiled his expansive smile. "Come again, Bowman," he said. "We gave you a good hoorawing, but it was all in fun. You know that, don't you?"

"Of course," Bowman said. "I couldn't prove a thing." He leaned forward and extended his open right hand. "I'll take your gun in place of mine, Kemp. Just in case there's an Indian left in Montana who hasn't heard that the game is up for Sword-Bearer."

Satterlee's smile held, but his eyes were murderous. He fumbled inside his shirt front and produced Bowman's own gun and handed it over. "Like I said, Bowman, come visit us again."

Bowman dropped the gun into his holster. "Maybe I will," he said coldly.

He reined his horse about; Jenny fell in to one side of him, Faro to the other, and they walked their horses across the clearing. The open way to the north was their direct route, but Jenny edged her mount north by west, obviously intending to reach timber sooner. Bowman's back was rigid with expectation; not until they were in the trees did he let himself relax. He smiled at Jenny. She had changed incredibly these last few minutes. With her bluff run, her shoulders now sagged, and weariness lined her face.

"How long were you out there?" he asked.

"All of last night," she said.

"I thought so. You followed Beale and the Indians from Hackett's?"

"Leading your horse along," she said. "I kept out of sight in the trees and watched the house until it was too dark to see. Thank heavens you left some food tied to your saddle. I saw Beale ride back this morning with Faro. I knew then that Beale had been sent to Broken Wagon."

"To get some orders from Ogden," Bowman said.

She nodded. "I was afraid to wait any longer then. Something was going on at Circle 6, and I had to know about it. When I rode up, I saw that your holster was empty. That looked bad. I took a chance that Satterlee would call off whatever game he was playing once I bought into it."

"And you bluffed, too, about that news about Sword-Bearer?"

"That came over the wire yesterday morning, just before I left camp. Satterlee's thoughts were mighty plain in his eyes. He could kill both you and me and blame it on to Indians. I think I guessed the same as you did when Beale showed up yesterday with those Indians. They're the same bunch who killed that man in camp the other night."

Bowman said, "You guessed right all along the line. I was to die this morning. Faro was to be implicated." He shook his head. "I'm damn' glad you didn't head back to camp as I told you to."

"No thanks are due to me," she said in her forthright way. "You'd better get one thing straight. Yesterday, when you told me only half your plan, I gave you only half my trust. I followed to see what you meant to do at Circle 6."

"You were afraid I might go to Satterlee

with a deal of some kind?"

"I simply don't know."

Faro had only been listening. Now he said, "We'd better be pushing harder than we are."

Bowman knew what the man feared. Where was the assurance that Satterlee might not put pursuit on their trail, with the thought of ambushing them along the way? Satterlee might come to such a notion, once he'd weighed all the factors. There was craftiness in the man, and there was also savage boldness. Bowman could hark up a picture of Satterlee at the head of his table, chewing on a cigar.

They rode through the early morning, a clear sky over them and the sun really showing to-day. They rode a world of tall trees and infrequent golden openness, jewelled pine needles and rocks aglitter with frost, bearing always towards the hill road. They galloped hard wherever the terrain permitted and walked their mounts through the more difficult passages. They held silent. By mid-morning they had struck the road to the hump, reaching at a point below where Bowman had turned off yesterday. At the first of the wide loops, they breathed their horses and looked back upon the stretch of country they had lately crossed.

Fatigue and reaction were catching up with Jenny. She sat slumped in her saddle. Bowman said softly, "We're almost home." He had thought himself long lost to tenderness until now.

Faro jerked up an arm and pointed. "Riders!" he cried. "Satterlee's Indians — ?"

Bowman, peering, discovered them, too, a half-dozen riders made so diminutive by distance that they might have been animated toys. Far below they rode, disappearing into timber, emerging again. Now and then he caught a flash of colour from their blankets. Indians, all right. But they were cutting towards the northeast, he noticed, at a tangent that would take them on up the Twosleep rather than to the foot of this hill. He thought he understood then.

"Satterlee's sent them away," he said. "He's afraid we've guessed nearly all the truth. If the law should come looking, there'll be no Indians at Circle 6. And he'll swear there never have been any."

Jenny said in a small voice, "Let them go."

Bowman knew what she meant, for he'd been thinking the same thing. Those vagabond Crees had blood on their hands, but he held no more grudge against them than he would have held against a knife while hating the man who wielded it. There was a whole history of one race betraying another with firewater and fancy promises, white man playing on the weakness of redskin. Where, then, should justice be meted out?

Faro said, "Another rider!" and pointed again.

It took Bowman a moment to locate this one. Far behind the Indians, a half-mile perhaps, a lone horseman came across a stretch of openness at a high gallop. Beale? Bowman couldn't be sure. He watched for a long time. The man seemed to be wearing a buffalo coat, but certainly he wasn't riding the same horse Beale had ridden yesterday. On the other hand, Beale would likely have changed mounts after his night ride to Broken Wagon. Bowman strained his eyes and grew more certain that it was Beale. He voiced this opinion.

"On his way back to Ogden to report," Jenny guessed.

Bowman gnawed his underlip thoughtfully as Beale became lost to sight in some trees. Finally Bowman said, "You two go on to camp. I'm going to wait here for Beale. I want to talk to him."

Jenny said, "Haven't you had enough?"

Bowman shook his head. "Beale could wind it up for us. It's worth trying anyway. Faro, take her along with you." He turned and looked at Faro then; they met each other's eyes squarely for the first time since they'd been in Circle 6's parlour. "And you, Faro? You'll be going back to the Imperial?"

Faro shrugged his fatalistic shrug. His long, thin face had turned unreadable. "Where else is there for me to go?"

"I think," Bowman said coldly, "I know what your choice would have been this morning."

Faro said, "I can't dispute you when I don't know myself what my choice would have been. I'm only grateful that Jenny came to save me from making a choice." Something of the spirit he'd shown on the stagecoach ride crept into his voice. "Besides, I don't see that you've proved yourself, Bowman."

Bowman said, "I'll not argue, either. Better get riding now. Both of you."

Jenny offered no objection. She was nearly spent; Bowman could see that plainly. What a long, cold night it must have been down there in the timber, he thought; and he smiled at her. She rode on with Faro, and Bowman listened to the diminishing beat of hoofs against the rocks of the road. He crooked a leg around his saddle horn and built himself a cigarette, finding it a sorry substitute for breakfast. He smoked and then jogged the roan closer to the inner edge of the road. Here he was concealed from anyone coming around the bend from below, and here he waited.

It was a long wait — so long that he finally decided that Beale had been riding towards some other destination and was not coming up the road. Nearly an hour had gone by when he heard the clop of hoofs against the road. He measured the progress of the oncoming rider by this sound and felt a tingle of excitement. He waited until the horseman was almost to the turn and then got his gun into his hand. He was thus when the rider appeared, and he said, "Hoist 'em up, Pete."

Beale's surprise was full blown and no pretty thing to see. He sat his saddle stupidly, not seeming to understand Bowman's order until Bowman repeated it. Then he raised his hands, cursing as he did so. Bowman rode close to him. Transferring his gun to his left hand, he reached under Beale's open buffalo coat, got

201

Beale's gun, and thrust it into the waist-band of his own trousers. Then he got Beale's saddle rope and shook out the loop and, fastening the man's wrists together, lashed them to the saddle horn. Beale began cursing again.

"Save your breath," Bowman advised him.

Leading Beale's horse with its trussed burden, he headed on up the road, hoping he'd meet no one along it. He climbed to the point where the steep trail he'd taken yesterday cut down towards Satterlee's. Now he'd finished out a full though jagged circle. He dropped down this trail into timber and then turned off at the point where he'd turned off before. Beale, spent with cursing, had lapsed into a sullen silence. Bowman began to look for remem-bered landmarks and at last came upon Sheep Creek. He followed it towards the Hackett place, and Beale broke silence as they rode into the clearing.

"What the hell do you think you're up to?" he demanded.

"Just looking for a quiet place where we can talk," Bowman said. He drew rein in the shadow of the two-story house.

Beale said, "You can pistol-whip me till you break the barrel of your gun, and you won't get anything out of me." He said this with a bold surety that didn't live in his eyes. Something had broken in the man.

Bowman swung down and stepped over to Beale and untied his hands. "Now why should I want to pistol-whip you, Pete?" He took Beale's gun from his waistband and dropped it into the foreman's holster. "There," Bowman said.

Beale stared unbelievingly at the gun. He almost reached for it, but changed his mind. He rubbed at his wrists. "You're turning me loose?"

"Why not?" Bowman said. "There's nothing between you and me, Pete."

"Not after this morning?" Beale's blocky face had drawn into a scowl of bewilderment. Violence this man could understand and meet; he had his own knack for dealing with tangibles. But here was something beyond Beale's experience. Bowman had counted on that.

"This morning?" Bowman said, and shrugged. "You were just standing by to carry out your boss's orders. I can appreciate loyalty in a man, Pete. Too bad Kemp isn't as loyal to you."

Beale's scowl darkened. "What do you mean by that?"

"Remember the stage station, the war whoops, the rifles banging, and Miles Hascomb going down? I carried the fight into the woods, you'll recall. There were moccasin tracks in the snow, and the booted tracks of a white man. And something else, Pete. A cigar that had been chewed but not smoked."

He had hoped this would hit Beale hard; it struck the man even harder than Bowman had expected. Just yesterday at this very place, he'd guessed that Beale would be a mighty angry man if he ever found himself duped. Anger now tightened Beale's jaw and built a blaze in his eyes. Then suspicion swept over him. "You're lying!" he said.

"Why should I?" Bowman countered. "Kemp has used those Indians time and again. First, he had them out there waiting for the stage to come. Then he used them to break into my room at Addisons' and steal a saddlebag. The empty bag is in yonder house, where it was dropped afterwards. Next he had them jump a man in Broken Wagon and knife and scalp him. That man was supposed to be me. You must have heard about that. Now he's sent those Indians packing because their usefulness has ended. In fact, it might be dangerous to have them found at the ranch. That's Kemp Satterlee for you. Once anybody's usefulness has ended, he heaves them out."

He walked to his horse and mounted and lifted his free hand. "So long, Pete."

"Wait!" Beale cried. "Are you trying to tell me Kemp was handling one of those rifles at the stage station?"

"No question about it," Bowman said. "He left his calling card when he left that chewed cigar. A man forgets that his habits brand him. Hell, he wanted Hascomb dead, didn't he? You'd gone to Helena on ranch business, so there was a chance you'd be on the same stage, but Kemp took that chance. What difference would it have made if you or I or Faro or the stage driver had stopped a bullet, too? Shooting at that range by moonlight, he might easily have dropped one of us by mistake. If it had been you, he'd have promoted somebody else to be foreman."

Beale looked stunned. He said slowly, "I'm minded that you said from the first that there was something queer about that Indian attack. They waited till the stage came, sure enough." He began to curse.

Bowman was casually turning his horse about; now he swung the mount back.

What was it, again, that Ben Hare had said about poker-playing?

"I know what you're thinking, Pete," Bowman said. "You're going to ride out. You're done with Kemp, now that you know what you know. But first you'd like to go and face him, gun to gun. Don't do it, Pete. The rest of his crew didn't have rifle bullets tossed at them. And they're still drawing his pay. They'd line up against you."

Beale said, "Just the same, I'm of a mind to chance it!"

"If you want to hit at him, there's a better way."

"You name it!"

"You were worried yesterday when you found me here. So was he. He knows the *Bugle* would like nothing better than to prove a partnership between him and Ogden on this beef contract business. What's hidden in this back country, Pete?"

Just for a moment Beale hesitated, suspicion strong in his eyes. But anger was there, too, the overpowering anger of a slow-thinking man. Then Beale said, "A herd wearing just about every brand in the Twosleep. Rustled cattle. A slaughterhouse. Wagons for toting the meat to Ogden's packing plant."

"I'd like a look at that layout from a safe distance," Bowman said. "Will you take me to it?"

Beale squinted. "So that's why you brought me here, to Hackett's!"

"Exactly," Bowman said. "The layout had to be somewhere close by or you wouldn't have been so worried yesterday. I've showed you my cards, Pete. I don't figure you owe me a thing. We can call it quits here and now, if you want. Or you can show me what I want to see. How about it?"

Beale took a moment to reach his decision. In that moment suspicion flared briefly again in his eyes, but his anger was stronger. He reined his mount about savagely. "Come along," he said. "I'll be riding that way anyway when I head out of this damn' country!"

CHAPTER THIRTEEN

Trouble in the Wind

Near dusk, Bowman dropped down the sharp switchbacks to Broken Wagon, the camp emerging below him, formless at first until one building after another became recognisable. A few lights were twinkling, like lost and fallen stars, by the time he hit the last turn, and there was a certain beauty to the scene, with the tree tops here and there, with the ugliness of the camp erased by the thronging shadows. But he was too tired to dwell on the picture twilight had wrought, too hungry to be interested in anything but getting his feet under a table. He had ridden the miles in triumph, but triumph had not eased the physical demands that now pressed him.

Light stood in the *Bugle* office window as he rode past the plant, and he glimpsed Jenny beyond the glass and saw that she was bent over her desk. He hoped she'd

208

found time to sleep during the day. Light had showed in the Addison place up the slope, too, and light now spilled from most of the buildings fronting on Placer. The planking was again thronged with men who went about their various businesses; voices eddied out of saloon and restaurant and hotel, and a blare of music beat from a hurdy-gurdy house. This had been a warmer day than the last; the snow was now nearly gone, and the mud had grown thicker and more pliable. Up on the south slope lanterns bobbed, where work was going forward on Ogden's packing plant. Already the building was far beyond the skeleton stage of yesterday morning. Hearing the tireless beat of the hammers, Bowman thought of what to-day had brought him and smiled.

He rode directly to the livery stable. The roan had earned a good rubdown and an extra ration of oats, and he instructed the hostler accordingly. The man, so talkative before, seemed unduly short to-night. Paying him, Bowman found that he was down to his last few dollars. By to-morrow, though, if all went well, he'd have no money worries. He touched the empty saddlebag he'd brought back from Hackett's place, then left it tied to the saddle.

Emerging to the planking, he stretched himself and worked his arms piston fashion, trying to get the stiffness out of his shoulders. Full dark now. He could see the lights of the restaurant where he'd eaten several times; but to reach it, he had to pass the saloon where he and Ben Hare had once drunk, and he turned into the place. One drink, he told himself. One drink to take some of the tension away before he ate.

Only a few miners were in the saloon, strangers to him, all of them, though he recognised Sam Marble by the man's plug hat and fancy waistcoat. The camp's founder was seated at a table with a couple of friends, a bottle and glasses before them as they listlessly played cards. Marble's whiskery face was slack, but the man didn't look fully drunk.

Talk fell away as Bowman walked towards the bar, and with the silence striking him, he was instantly alert. He turned and ran his eyes around the room and caught all of them watching him; they at once dropped their eyes. He was tired enough so that their attitude irritated him. The hostler, too, had acted oddly. He wondered if the word had got out that he was a pardoned convict and thus he'd become a man of special interest. Who'd done the talking? Ogden, or Hare — or both?

He walked to the bar and said, "Whisky."

The barkeep placed a bottle and glass before him, and Bowman poured a drink. The barkeep made himself very busy cleaning imaginary spots off the counter. Bowman watched him for a while. The man became aware of his stare and turned his back and found a glass and began polishing it.

Bowman asked, "What the hell is wrong with me?"

The barkeep faced him. "Trouble in the wind for you, friend," he said stolidly.

"I haven't been back in camp fifteen minutes."

"But you rode along Placer coming in, which gave everybody a chance to spot you. The word's got around."

Bowman upped his drink and took it fast. The whisky hit the emptiness in his stomach hard and lay there like a burning coal. "Trouble!" he said and laughed. "Hell, man, I've *had* trouble! What special brand you got for me around camp?"

Then he knew. The barkeep's face had suddenly lost its stolidity; the barkeep was gazing over Bowman's shoulder towards the door, and now the man dropped down behind the counter. The glass he'd been polishing crashed against the floor.

Bowman didn't have to turn around. In the bar mirror he could see the man who stood framed in the doorway, and he could see the gun held waveringly in the man's hand. Chairs scraped and boots clattered as men hastily moved themselves away from the centre of the room. Someone — Sam Marble — spoke a name, but Bowman didn't need to hear it. He recognised those burning, compelling eyes, that spiky black beard. He recognised them because he'd seen Jud Addison's picture.

"Bowman!" Addison called. "I know you're here!" His eyes ran over the room, then followed every man's gaze to Bowman's back. "You wife-snatching pack rat. Turn around and take it in the guts!"

Bowman turned. As in that dread moment before Circle 6's ranch house early this morning, he wondered if his muscles would respond to what he must now demand of them. He turned; but as he did so, he grasped the whisky bottle from the bar and flung it at Addison. The bottle grazed the man's shoulder. Addison's gun exploded; Bowman heard the bar mirror shatter. Addison came charging across the

212

room towards him, a stocky, stumbling figure.

Bowman didn't try for his own gun. He rushed to meet Addison's charge, and the man clubbed at him with the gun. Addison was drunk, crazy drunk. Bowman smashed at him with a fist. He got through to Addison's jaw, and the force of the blow shook Addison hard enough so that the gun dropped from his hand. Bowman kicked the gun across the floor. Addison was cursing wildly. He clawed at Bowman; he tried to wrap his arms around Bowman. Bowman kept free of him and struck at the man with his fists. Addison went down into a shuddering heap.

Bowman stood over him. His chest was heaving, and he had to fight for air. He wondered if there were strength enough in him to meet the test if Addison came to his feet. Lifting his fists had been like lifting all the miles he'd ridden to-day. Then he realised that Addison was sobbing wildly, and Bowman swept a hand before his eyes and saw the man then as something other than a drunken brute, murder bent.

He looked down at Addison and said, "You poor devil!"

Sam Marble moved out from the wall. "He come into camp looking like he hadn't

213

eat for a week. Somebody told him what was bound to be told him, and he started liquoring." He turned to the miners who'd been seated at the table with him and gestured towards Addison. "Lock him up till he's sober and over the notion of doing harm." He picked up Addison's gun from the floor and stowed it in his pocket, then looked at Bowman again. "I ain't sure but what in his place I'd have tried the same thing."

Bowman said wearily, "What he didn't know was that he didn't have anything to worry about."

He walked out of the place. He stood in the coolness of the night, and shock hit him as he remembered how close that bullet had come. He began to tremble. He willed himself to steadiness and walked resolutely to the restaurant and went inside. A number of men were here. The same silence fell that had fallen in the saloon, and he looked about him and said distinctly, "Addison is on his way to jail. It's all over. You can quit waiting like a damn' bunch of buzzards for the kill!"

He took a table and closed all of them out of his thinking. He ordered and ate, had a cigarette, and it seemed a better world then. He was sorry for his outburst.

He remembered that the barkeep had been about to warn him when Addison had walked in. He thanked the barkeep in his mind and reflected that somebody was going to have to pay for a bar mirror. Still, the whole business had taken the edge from the triumph he had felt on the ride back from the Twosleep. He could hear Jud Addison sobbing in the sawdust on a saloon floor.

"Somebody told him what was bound to be told him," Sam Marble had said. Somebody? Anybody. Ogden, perhaps.

He went from the restaurant, heading along Placer towards the *Bugle* plant. The night was almost mild, and he wondered how many degrees the temperature had risen in the last few days. He had just had Sig Ogden in his thoughts, and now he saw Ogden walking towards him, breasting the tide of humanity that flowed and eddied upon the planking, a tall, stooped man with a shawl over his shoulders. He would have passed Ogden, but the man stared at him and broke stride and said, "Good-evening." If Bowman's presence had surprised him, Ogden's bony face did not show it.

Bowman said, "I must be quite a disappointment to you. First there was Kemp

Satterlee's gun, but I managed to get past it. Then there was Jud Addison, but you've probably heard how he made out."

Ogden said, "The word has got around that Jud's been jailed. I'm glad there was no bloodshed."

"You're a liar, Sig."

Ogden shook his head, his face sad. "My future lies in this camp. I've too much at stake to be mixed into petty violences. Will you ever learn that?"

Anger swept through Bowman. "You sicken me, Sig. I've already told you that all of your breed sickens me. In your own minds, you're empire builders, colonisers, or pioneers, so exalted that you can forgive your left hand everything it does. You speak of futures, when the only future that concerns you is your own. You mouth a lofty estimate of yourself so often that it becomes reality to you. You give yourself every name but the right one — scoundrel."

Ogden turned cold and remote, as he had at their first meeting. "Small men always hate big men," he said. "It's something I observed long ago. Whatever it is eating at you, Bowman, I trust that some day you'll overcome it."

Bowman said, "Who knows? Maybe that

day will be to-morrow."

He brushed on past Ogden and strode towards the *Bugle* plant. He came in and closed the door behind him and Jenny came out of her chair and stood with her lips slightly parted. The thing he saw in her eyes he'd seen in the eyes of men when word had come to Deer Lodge that they were free because a governor had scratched his name on a piece of paper. Hers was a joy too big to be grasped quickly.

She said, "Neil — !"

"It's all over and neither of us was hurt," he said, though he knew this wasn't exactly true.

"We hadn't been back to camp two hours when the word started going up and down the street like a grass fire. Jud Addison was back. I thought of waiting at the bottom of the hill till you showed up. But I might have had to wait forever. I thought of everything — and could do nothing. Nothing but hope."

He walked towards her and put his hands to her shoulders and shook her slightly. "It's all over," he said again. "There are more important things to think about. Is Ben here?"

"In the back room," she said.

"Call him," he said. "Now I've got some writing to do."

He took her chair before the desk and pawed around till he found paper and pen. He began writing, scribbling furiously. He heard her call Ben Hare's name through the connecting doorway; he heard the printer shuffle into the office. He didn't look up; he kept writing. When he'd finished a page, he passed it over his shoulder to Jenny and went on with a second page. He heard her sharp intake of breath as she read, and then the rustle of paper as she handed it to Ben Hare. He finished a second page and a third and passed these along. Then he flung down the pen and swung the swivel chair about.

Jenny looked up from the sheet she held. "A slaughterhouse on upper Sheep Creek," she said. "A herd of stolen cattle. Everything."

"Yes," he said, "and a statement from Pete Beale about a dozen meetings between Ogden and Satterlee, here and in the Twosleep. It's written on a scrap of paper with a stub of pencil, but I've got Beale's signature, bold as brass."

Ben Hare said, "Yes, but have you got Beale?"

"He'll be around Dillon for the next few

weeks, if I want him. He told me where I could send him money if he's to make the trip back."

Hare glanced at the paper he held and ran a hand through his mouse-coloured hair, standing it on end. He pursed his lips and squinted his eyes almost shut and said, "Verily, here are words headier than wine, exciting to the soul and tasty to the tongue. Methinks this is where the lid blows off."

Bowman stood up. "I want that set in type by tomorrow morning and ready for the front page. You'll work all night if you have to, Ben. Whatever we pay you, you'll be paid double if the front page form is locked and ready for the press when I show up here at breakfast time. Now I'm going to get some sleep."

He stepped towards the door. Jenny said, "Wait," and grasped him by the arm. "How did you learn all this?"

"By telling Pete Beale who killed Miles Hascomb. And by pointing out how easily he could have died that same night."

She took this without flinching, though some of the colour left her face. "Then it was Satterlee and his Indians at the stage station, too."

"Yes," he said. "He left sign behind him. I read that sign again at Circle 6. You guessed right about how that bummer died. But that was the second time Satterlee had seen a way to hide a murder behind the Indian scare."

Her eyes had turned bleak. "Whatever Satterlee did, Ogden was in on it. Both of them are going to pay for those murders."

"To-morrow," Bowman said. "To-morrow they pay." He took a step towards the door.

"You won't be going back to that house," she said, and she looked in the direction of the Addison place.

"Only for to-night."

He left the office. He strode along Placer and turned off at the cross street where he began his climb to the house on the slope. He supposed that the door might be barred; but as he raised his hand to knock, Helen opened it for him. He knew that she heard his footsteps and that she'd been waiting for footsteps. By lamplight he read on her face the toll the waiting had taken. She looked a dozen years older than when he'd last seen her. She put out her hands blindly, and he was afraid she was going to fall. He caught her in his arms and steadied her.

"Jud's in jail," he said. "No harm was done."

She moved away from him. She closed the door, putting her back to it, and raised a hand to push nervously at her hair. "But once he's out, he'll come looking for you," she said. "There'll be no end of it until one of you is dead."

He shook his head. "He'd heard a lot of lies about me. He'd soaked them in whisky. But he's no killer. He fired one shot when he could have fired six. The last I saw of him, he was crying."

She only stared at him numbly. "There'll be no end to it until one of you is dead," she repeated. "And no matter which one of you it is, I'll be to blame."

"No," he insisted. "He's made his try. You told me about his pride. He tried to buy back a small piece of it to-night, but the price was too high for him. He's no killer."

She made a feeble motion with her hands. "Just the same, he's lost to me. Oh, how I hate this house!"

"He's not lost, if you face up to a choice," he said. "It's very simple. Either it's this" — he swept his hand to take in the whole house — "or it's the way you'll have to live if you're to share his life. You had that choice once. I think you could have it again."

Turning, he went on to his room. He lighted the lamp and got his gun belt and boots off, then fell upon the bed. Later, he told himself, he'd get his clothes off and blow out the lamp. Weariness was a drug in him, but the trouble was that it hadn't drugged his mind.

To-morrow, he kept thinking. To-morrow he'd put into effect the second half of his plan, the half he hadn't told Jenny about in the Twosleep yesterday. This thought should have brought him his greatest sense of triumph, but it didn't. He tried to push the whole business from his mind, but it persisted. Then he heard the soft tapping at the window. Instantly he rolled out of the bed to the floor on the far side of the window. He got hold of his gun. He looked towards the lamp, wondering if he should shoot it out.

He heard his name whispered at the window, and raising his head a little, he saw the black outline of a man beyond the glass and thought he caught the glint of starlight on a gun barrel.

"Neil!" the voice spoke again. "Open up, or I'll smash out the window! Blow out the lamp and open up!"

He'd had, Bowman thought, more than enough for one day. There was no reserve strength left in him for what he had to face. But it was there to be faced, and no changing that fact. He arose, walked to the lamp and blew it out, and then went to the window and unfastened it and raised the glass.

"Climb in, Bart," he said.

CHAPTER FOURTEEN

The Deadline

In Sig Ogden, as he continued along Placer after meeting Bowman, the knowledge was strong that he had come out second best in the encounter. Damn Bowman and his flaying tongue! Bowman had a kink in him, of course, but just the same Ogden kept turning their talk over and over in his mind. The accusation still stung. Bowman had as good as told him that he knew Sig Ogden to be the trigger for Kemp Satterlee's gun. And then Bowman had laid a name to him. "Scoundrel." But the words that persisted most sharply in Ogden's thinking were Bowman's last words, his reference to to-morrow. Held up for consideration, those words made little sense; yet they'd implied a threat and been spoken with a surety that troubled Ogden.

To-morrow — ? Now what in the name of blazes did Bowman plan to do to-morrow?

To-day had been bad enough. Ogden had lived most of the day in anticipation that had yielded nothing. Looking back now, he realised that from noon on he expected Pete Beale to come riding to camp to seek him out surreptitiously to tell him that Bowman was dead. But Beale hadn't come. Instead, Faro had ridden in with the Hascomb girl. Ogden had seen them from a window of the Imperial, and worry had tugged at him. Now what had Jenny Hascomb been doing over the hump, and how had she and Faro come to be journeying together? Ben Hare might have been able to tell him, but Ben hadn't shoved his wicked old face into the Imperial to-day. Ogden had begun to fret. He'd thought it quite a stroke of inspiration to send Faro to Circle 6 last night, but obviously things hadn't worked out as planned. Had Satterlee been careless again? How many times did he have to warn Kemp to be careful, careful!

Still, he'd kept telling himself, Neil Bowman hadn't ridden back. But that fact hadn't kept him from continuing to fret all afternoon. Then word got around that Jud Addison had returned. Interesting news, that. Mighty interesting. Yet it hadn't been Sig Ogden who told Addison about the man who'd moved into the house on the slope. No need. Some busybody had taken care of that. Good enough! Let Bowman escape Satterlee and there'd be Jud Addison awaiting him. Addison had prowled morosely from saloon to saloon and done some of his afternoon's drinking at the Imperial. Ogden had told his barkeeps not to charge the man. Smart business to contribute a little fuel to the fire, he thought.

But what in hell was keeping Pete Beale?

Ogden had taken his supper in his quarters and been at the meal when one of his housemen had brought him a new report. Neil Bowman was in camp and had run up against Jud Addison. Ogden prided himself that he'd shown no expression as he listened. So Jud Addison had had his moment and ended up in jail. Neil Bowman had walked free from the Twosleep and now walked free again, safe from Addison. Did Bowman wear some sort of charm that kept him so damnably lucky?

Ogden had sat, turning the situation over in his mind, his worries growing. Suddenly he wanted to be out of the Imperial, to pace a wider space than the saloon provided.

Passing from the Imperial, he noticed

Faro at his table dealing cards. For a moment he thought of calling Faro to his office; but as he stood studying Faro's blank face, he decided against trying to talk to the man. Something had gone wrong in the Twosleep — terribly wrong — and Faro must certainly know the whys and wherefores. But since Bowman walked free, then obviously Faro had not been implicated in a murder, and thus Faro also walked free — free as his spirit permitted. But there could be dangerous depths to Faro. Prod the gambler again, and one might prod a sleeping tiger. Instinct told Ogden to leave well enough alone.

And so he had come to the street and chanced upon Bowman, and now he walked on.

Seldom seen beyond his saloon, he knew that his departure from regular routine must be exciting curiosity. Well, a man could walk the street if he wished. From the doorway of a restaurant, Sam Marble wished him a gruff good-evening. Ogden schooled his face against showing worry, nodded, and walked on, to all appearances merely taking an evening stroll. When he had gone as far as Placer would take him, there was nothing to do but turn around and walk back.

Sam Marble was no longer in the restaurant doorway. Others spoke to Ogden, though, and he acknowledged their greetings with dignity. He had gained respect here, and he weighed this for what it was, an asset good at the Helena banks when he wished to expand. He had many plans, he reminded himself, and any kind of capital counted.

He walked with this dreaming until he was nearly opposite the Imperial and could see its lighted front diagonally across from him. He was now abreast of a log building that had once been somebody's cabin but had since been converted into a bakery. He put his shoulders to the wall and leaned here, his arms folded.

Clearly to him came the beat of hammers and the rasp of saws from the packing plant up on the south slope, and clear to his vision were the lights of the Imperial across the way. These things, and more, were at stake. He remembered the other boom camps he'd known before Broken Wagon; he had pursued his own gods of fortune in those camps and achieved his own small successes, but they'd never been enough. Always one essential truth had been plain to him, and always the ability to capitalise on it had been beyond his eager fingertips. It was not the muckers who emerged rich over the long pull, he observed. One man started a sawmill, another opened a freighting line, and still another built a stamp mill, and these were the farsighted ones who ended up with the miners' gold. These were the big names in the Territory to-day. Soon his could be such a name, but there was Bowman's threat to remember.

One man who stood between Sig Ogden and his ambitions. One man. Now all the worries of this long day of worry swirled up to engulf Ogden and turn him desperate. He had urged Satterlee again and again to be careful, but there had to be a day when the bold stroke was the telling stroke.

To-morrow probably. . . .

Bart Carney, Bowman noticed, kept his gun in his hand as he climbed through the bedroom window. Bowman still held his own gun laxly, but once Carney was in the room, he thrust the gun into his waistband and put both hands to closing the window against the night's chill. No sense trying to match Carney's gun skill, Bowman told himself wearily. This decision was part of a sense of futility that had grown upon him ever since he realised it was Carney calling to him.

He turned and faced the old he-wolf in the gloom. "Put your gun away, Bart," he said. "I've had all the fight I want for one day."

Carney said gruffly, "It's the money I'm after, Neil. Just fork it over and I'll be gone."

Bowman could make out the lean figure, but Carney's face was only a smudge and so beyond reading. The surprising thing was that Carney's voice held neither anger nor threat; the man sounded tired and almost sad. Even more surprising to Bowman was his own reaction. He had known this moment would come — known it from the time Ben Hare had told him that Bart Carney was free of Deer Lodge. He, Bowman, had been a hunted man ever since, hearing Carney's hoofbeats on the back trail. Yet now that Carney had come, it was like meeting an old friend, except that there was a thing between them that sullied the friendship. Carney had just put it into words. The money. The damn' money!

Shaking his head, Bowman asked, "How did you find me, Bart?"

"You left broad tracks, boy. They led down to the stage road. I flipped a coin then. Helena or Broken Wagon? The coin sent me to this camp. I risked showing myself on the street long enough to ask a few questions. And when I saw your lamp burning, I peeked in your window. Now how about that money, Neil?"

"It's gone, Bart. Stolen the first day I hit camp."

"Stolen!"

"That's right."

Bowman expected wrath now, but Carney only laughed, the sound low and deep throated. "I stole it from a stage-coach. You stole it from me, and then somebody stole it from you. Is that the straight of it?"

Bowman nodded.

"You got an idea who?"

"I know who."

A sharp edge came to Carney's voice. "Then spit out his name!"

"No," Bowman said. "You'd go after him. To-night likely. He's my meat."

There it lay. Queer, Bowman thought, but this was just like being back in Deer Lodge, the two of them talking in darkness and keeping their voices low so the guards wouldn't hear. How many nights had they

231

done this? And what had it forged between them? Something, surely. Something that made them not wholly enemies, even now. Something almost as big as twenty thousand dollars, but not quite.

Carney's face was becoming clearer in the gloom. He looked puzzled. "How did you find my cache in the first place, Neil?"

"You talked in your sleep, Bart. I led you on. I got the whole story from you."

"That's what I finally decided," Carney said. He shook his head. "I thought better of you, boy."

Bowman winced. "I thought better of myself — once."

"Going to tell me who got that money?"

"No, Bart."

"Then what choice do you leave me?" Carney asked angrily. "I've tried remembering that in stealing it you did no worse than I did before you. I've tried remembering that we were friends. But I'm not riding out of this camp without the money. Are you telling it straight about its being stolen? They told me to-day you'd bought an interest in the newspaper here."

"That took five thousand. The rest got stolen. I'll have it back to-morrow."

"You'd better tell me how, Neil."

"I'm selling the newspaper to the man

who stole the money. I'm making him pay a high price for it. I'm pinching him where I've itched to pinch him all along — in the purse. I'll have your money for you to-morrow."

"Blackmail?" Carney asked.

Again Bowman winced. "What difference what it's called? The score gets settled."

Carney became a silent, thoughtful shadow in an old blanket coat; and Bowman waited him out, wondering if now the showdown would come. Odd that he didn't really care.

Carney stepped towards the window. "You struck me as a straight kid once," he said. "Somewhere you got your twine tangled. The same could be said for me. Damned if I'm not sorry for you, Neil." He paused. "Just below camp, as you come in on the Helena road, there's an old cabin in a grove of trees to your right. You know the place?"

"I saw it as I came in the first morning," Bowman said.

"I'll wait there till sundown to-morrow," Carney said. He hoisted the window sash and threw a leg over the sill. "You'll come to me there, and you'll have twenty thousand dollars in your fist. Don't forget to show up, Neil. Don't make me come after you."

Carney was gone then. Bowman closed the window and stood for a long time in the darkness of the room. Then he stretched himself out on the bed again. He took the gun from his waistband and laid it on the floor. He thought of Carney moving with wolf wariness through the night; he thought of the deadline Carney had named.

How long had the man been here? Ten minutes? Fifeen? Everything had changed in that time. No, nothing had changed. Hadn't he meant all along to face Sig Ogden to-morrow and bend Ogden to his will? Hadn't that been the other half of the scheme, the part he hadn't told Jenny Hascomb about?

He stirred restlessly in the darkness and asked himself how he had come to this place and this moment, and now the truth stood stark. It had begun in a courtroom in the Yellowstone Valley with Sherm Wheeler combing his red whiskers with his fingers and hiding a smile behind his hand. He had hated Sherm Wheeler and had seen in Sig Ogden a chance to strike back at Wheeler. Yes, at all the Wheelers of the world, for they were all cut from the same cloth. He had lost sight of everything but that goal. And now there was no choice for him because Bart Carney would be waiting. That was where the irony lay. A short while ago he'd been wondering about the choice he made, but now there was no choice.

He rolled over and wished that he could go to sleep. The hell with bothering to get the rest of his clothes off! Then he heard a gentle tapping at the door and Helen Addison calling his name.

"What is it?" he asked.

"Neil, are you all right? I thought I heard voices in your room."

"I'm alone," he said. "There's nothing to worry about. Go back to bed."

But still he didn't hear the whisper of her feet moving away from the door. After a long moment, she said, "Neil — ?"

"Yes."

"I've thought over what you said about the choice I'll have to make. I know now what I'm going to do."

"That's good," he said.

She didn't speak again, and he began to slip off into sleep. He thought, she knows what she's going to do, and I know what I have to do, and he almost laughed at the way things had turned out. Bart Carney, he remembered, had felt sorry for him. Damn it, he was beginning to feel sorry for himself. The hell with it! He wished that to-morrow were here and over; and wishing that, he fell asleep.

CHAPTER FIFTEEN

Surprise Alarm

While the morning was still young, Bowman came into the *Bugle* office and found Jenny at her desk and Ben Hare making a clatter in the back room. After breakfast, Bowman had gone to the livery stable and got the empty saddlebag he fetched from Hackett's. He dropped the bag on the littered table where job printing stood heaped, and nodded to Jenny. "Ben got that story set up?"

She brought her chair about and regarded him questioningly, and he realised that he sounded very abrupt.

"Ben worked all night, Neil," she said. "The form for the front page is locked up and ready for the press."

Bowman thrust his head through the connecting doorway. "Ben, draw me a proof of the front page."

Hare looked up from a fount where he'd

been redistributing some type. He was in a high mood for one who'd put in so much work. "To-night is press night," he said. "But give me a brimming cup of the elixir that sustaineth, my impatient friend, and I'll hand you a printed edition in a few more hours."

"Just draw a proof," Bowman insisted. He was about to turn from the doorway but was swung back by an alarming thought. "Understand one thing, Ben. You're not to run off the edition till you get an order from me."

Hare raised his eyebrows, but made no comment. He went about inking the form and drawing a proof. He brought the moist page to Bowman, who saw that the story scribbled off so hastily last night held the most important place on the page. The stepladder of headlines composed by Hare suited Bowman. He ran his eye down them. OGDEN'S PERFIDY PROVED — SLAUGHTERHOUSE IN THE TWOSLEEP — RUSTLED BEEF TO FEED BROKEN WAGON — SATTERLEE A SILENT PARTNER.

"Fine!" Bowman said. He carefully folded the proof so that it would not smear and placed it inside the saddlebag. He was aware that Hare was watching him closely.

Taking the saddlebag, he strode from the office and cut diagonally across the street towards the Imperial.

He had not so much as glanced at Jenny as he departed. He hadn't dared to. All his movements had been equally abrupt this morning. He had gone from the Addison place to the restaurant and thence to the livery stable and the *Bugle* plant like some sort of machine wound up and put in motion. Right foot, left foot. Mustn't tarry to think, he had kept telling himself. Mustn't dwell on any consequence save the consequence if he did not keep rendezvous with Bart Carney at the camp's outskirts before sundown. Mustn't, above all, give Jenny a chance to ask him what he planned to do. First the deed and then the explanation. Only by such a procedure could he keep himself from faltering.

Sunshine to-day, and warmth, as though Indian summer had been wooed back from some hiding place where she had dwelt this last snowy week. Better to think about the weather, he told himself, or anything but what the next hour would hold. Only a few people on the planking so early. Yonder stood the jail building, and he remembered Jud Addison. How had Jud fared last night, and how sour had the dawn looked to him?

Helen Addison hadn't been about when he left the house this morning. He wondered what Helen had decided to do.

His mind forced to these things, he strode into the Imperial.

Almost empty, the place seemed bigger. Chairs were stacked upon the tables, their upturned legs making a naked sort of forest. An old swamper worked listlessly, and no man stood behind the bar, and no customer was here. The place smelled stale; it had, Bowman thought, the smell of sin. His bootsteps echoed as he crossed the room to the stairs leading up to Ogden's office. He climbed the stairs, opened the door unceremoniously, and stepped in.

Ogden was in his captain's chair before his desk. Ogden had heard the boots on the stairs but evidently hadn't guessed who his visitor would be, for he showed surprise. "What is this, Bowman?"

"Business," Bowman said. "The deal you tried to make."

Ogden said, "The only deal we ever discussed was my buying the *Bugle*."

"That's what I mean, Sig."

Ogden's bony face showed no elation, but rather a guarded wariness. "You mean you intend to sell?"

"If the price is right. Read this first and

240

decide for yourself."

He opened the saddlebag and got out the page proof and handed it to Ogden. Ogden picked a pair of steel-rimmed spectacles from his desk, placed them on his nose, spread out the proof, and began reading. It was a moment in which the silence held so hard that Bowman could hear the rasp of the swamper's mop against the floor downstairs. And it was a moment, Bowman realised, that should have held full triumph but fell a good deal short of that.

Ogden read on, his face tightening. Damned if he didn't have to admire the man, Bowman thought. Ogden was seeing his whole world crumble, yet he kept his face stiff. His hands trembled, though, as he placed the proof on the desk. "What is your price?" he asked hoarsely.

"There's unfinished business first," Bowman said. He tossed the saddlebag at Ogden; it struck the man's chest hard and fell to the floor. "There was fifteen thousand dollars in that bag, Sig. Remember? And a pardon from the governor. Put back what you stole."

Ogden stared down at the bag. Beneath his stiff surface the man was terribly shaken, Bowman knew. Ogden was making a fight with himself. He shuddered; his hands opened and closed, and then he reached and picked up the bag. "Very well," he said. He got up and walked to the bedroom doorway and brushed the curtain aside. Bowman came right behind him. Ogden knelt before the safe. He began fumbling with the dial. On top of the safe lay a Colt .45.

Bowman picked up the gun and tossed it on to the bed. "Not that using it would have done you any good," Bowman said. "If I don't walk out of here, Ben Hare will have the paper on the street before long."

Ogden looked up at him, temper standing in his eyes. "Now will he?"

"I wouldn't risk otherwise, if I were you," Bowman said.

Ogden got the safe open and pawed into it. He brought out packets of currency and at last a folded sheet of paper. "There," he said.

Bowman glanced at the paper to make sure it was the pardon. He stowed it in his coat pocket. The currency he scooped up and put into the saddlebag. "So you were bluffing the other night," he said. "You had the money here all the time."

"I was bluffing," Ogden admitted. He stood up and brushed at his knees. "I had

Kemp's Indians force their way into Addisons' the afternoon of Miles's funeral; afterwards I told them to get the empty saddlebag out of camp. My idea was to get something on you. There's one thing I want you to know, Bowman; it was not my notion that Hascomb be cut down. Or that man on the slope who was supposed to be you."

"No," Bowman said, "that would be more in Satterlee's line. You didn't want the blood on your hands; you just wanted the benefit. You were also intending to let somebody else do the killing night before last when you sent Satterlee word to see that I didn't come back from the Twosleep. Yes, you've kept your hands clean. I wonder how your conscience looks."

The corners of Ogden's lips quirked. "You've got your money back, Bowman. You can spare me the sermon. What is the rest of your price?"

"Forty thousand dollars," Bowman said.

Ogden flinched as though he'd been struck. "Forty thousand! That's a great deal more than the paper's worth!"

"It all depends," Bowman said. "The question is what it's worth to you. Just think it over, and you'll agree that forty thousand might be cheap."

Again temper swept through Ogden. It shook him as the wind shakes a tree, but there was strong discipline in him. Bowman wondered how many towns had strengthened that discipline, how many past storms had assailed it. He watched the fight in Ogden and saw the surrender in the man's eyes.

"I don't keep that kind of money here, Bowman."

"But you can get it."

"Part of it," Ogden said. "All but my ready cash is in the safe at the Wells Fargo office. It's a stronger safe than mine."

Bowman said, "You'll borrow the rest, if you have to. You'll have forty thousand dollars over at the *Bugle* office by noon. I'll be waiting there. And if you forget to show up, the paper goes to press."

He turned to move out of the room, and Ogden said in a strangled voice, "This is blackmail, you know."

"Yes, I know," Bowman said. "You're not the first to give it that name."

He walked from the room. He came down the stairs and saw that the swamper had got most of the chairs off the tables. Behind his faro bank sat Faro, who must have come in since Bowman had entered. An odd hour for Faro to be here. The gambler looked up at Bowman and nodded only slightly, then dropped his eyes, not speaking. He looked old and tired; his face was blank.

Bowman came out on to the planking and stood there, the saddlebag heavy in his hand. He looked along the street and saw Helen Addison walking slowly, her back to him. She'd be shopping at the mercantile, he supposed. He registered this with no more real interest than he had had in Faro's presence in the Imperial. His mind was still on what had passed between himself and Ogden. He ran his free hand against his thigh as though he were rubbing dirt from it. He looked at his hand, then rubbed it again. Here was the hour he had awaited ever since he'd first heard of Ogden, though his full plan had formed itself later. Here was the blow dealt to all the Sherm Wheelers and the Sig Ogdens and their ilk. Here was success to all his planning, but still he found it empty.

He shook his head. He'd had no choice, he reminded himself. Especially not since Bart Carney had crawled through his window last night. No, it went back farther than that. He'd chosen a path when he'd fashioned the harsh philosophy that had taken him into the hills to the buried loot that had never belonged to him, and this was where the trail had led him, to here and now.

He shouldn't be thinking, he reminded himself. He ought to keep moving woodenly, mechanically, just as he'd been moving all morning. Right foot, left foot. Right foot, left foot. He had to cross the street and go through with the last phase of this. He had to go and tell Jenny Hascomb now. But still he stood. The swamper came out of the Imperial and brushed past him with the air of one bent upon important business. Bowman watched the fellow scurry along the street and accost Sam Marble, who was coming out of the restaurant. Bowman hefted the saddlebag. Get moving, he thought.

He crossed over and came into the *Bugle* plant. He dropped the weighted saddlebag on the table and avoided Jenny's eyes as he stepped to the doorway and called Ben. The printer came shuffling into the office.

Bowman said, "I've just talked to Ogden. He'll be here by noon. With forty thousand dollars. I've sold him the *Bugle*."

Ben Hare said, "Well, I'll be tee-double-damned," but it was at Jenny that Bowman was finally looking.

He hadn't known what to expect from

Jenny when the news broke. It was one of those things he hadn't dared speculate about. She sat in the swivel chair, her hands in her lap, her eyes big and sombre and vacant; it struck him hard that this was exactly as she'd looked when he'd first seen her, weighted down by grief over her father's death. Now she shook her head slowly. Speech trembled on her lips and at last came.

"So you were the enemy after all," she said.

"No!" he protested. "I've simply done what's best. If the paper comes out, Ogden will be packed and gone from here. We can't bring him to court for what happened to Miles Hascomb. He's already taken pains to put the blame on to Kemp Satterlee. And Satterlee will blame it on the Indians. Beale couldn't testify to the contrary on that score. I tell you, I've just got Ogden where he can be hurt most." He looked at Hare. "I told you I was going to pinch him in the purse."

Hare said, "You really think you have the right to sell the paper?"

"In black and white," Bowman said. "I made a point of that when I dickered with Miles. I can dispose of the property as long as doing so is in the best interests of my

247

partner. Who's to judge?" He swung his eyes to Jenny. "This is no place for you, no life for you. To-morrow or next week or next month another Ogden will roll into camp with another quick-money scheme. And the paper will have to make the same old fight all over again."

Jenny said hollowly, "Of course. Do you suppose I haven't known that? That doesn't change the way I feel!"

"You'd stay here and fight one Ogden after another?"

"I'd stay here," she said. "That's all I've wanted. I told you as much in the Two-sleep. If only you'd listened! I'm tired of running."

Bowman turned to Hare. "Show her the sense of what I've done," he begged. "It's the main chance for all of us. You talked of the main chance a few days ago."

Hare shook his head. "Trouble is, I half believed what I said, too. I've even taken Ogden's filthy money and his prime whisky to act as spy for him."

Jenny looked up, startled.

"That surprises you?" Hare asked. "Let me assure you that I've also been loyal to my bread and butter. I've made a game out of giving Ogden only such information as would have been camp property within a

few hours anyway. Yet I confess to strad-
dling the fence. It was my thought that
when a real choice had to be made, I
would reach a decision. Verily, the time
seems to have come."

Bowman said, "And you win either way.
Ogden will want to run the paper once he's
bought it. He'll need you."

Hare sighed, "I've set up many stories in
my time. The first news of gold in Cali-
fornia. The firing on Fort Sumter. The
assassination of Lincoln. Good news and
bad. Big stories and little ones. All of them
happening somewhere far away, none of
them really bearing on my own whisky-
soaked life. Last night I set up my biggest
story. Don't you see, it was about what was
happening in my own town and likely
involving my own filthy hide. So that, it
appears, must have been the main chance I
was really waiting for, in spite of the
whisky talk I once made to you, my friend.
Oh, what a story we've got!"

Bowman looked at him, seeing the man
clearly for the first time. "You mean you'd
put the paper on the street?"

"I am a poor example of my craft," Ben
Hare said. "But if my veins carry fifty per
cent alcohol, the other half is printer's ink.
Given the choice, I would say be-damned

to Ogden and his forty thousand smelly dollars. Yes, I want to see the paper hit the street."

"And you shall, Ben," Jenny said. "I'm not sure that a court would grant this man the right to sell more than his half interest. I'm not concerned with the legality. If I have to, I'll stand in the doorway with a gun to keep Ogden off the premises while you get the presswork done. We're putting out our paper to-day."

"I'm beaten," Bowman thought.

He couldn't tell them of Bart Carney, who waited and would come hunting him if the rendezvous were not kept. Carney was his own problem. But thinking of the man, he saw one last loophole for himself. Sell back his interest in the *Bugle* to Jenny, and there'd be five thousand to add to the fifteen thousand in the saddlebag. Carney would have his money, and Ogden could be defied. Bowman shook his head. That would leave him empty handed. He'd lived too long with a debt to collect to give up the idea of collecting from Ogden. He said desperately, "I put in four years in Deer Lodge for something I didn't do. Ben can tell you that. I've got something coming for those years."

"Yes, Ben told me," Jenny said. "It didn't

matter to me that you'd been in prison. I couldn't believe that it would really matter to you. Everyone's wagon breaks down sometime or other. Some never get back on the road on which they were headed. The weak ones sit in the wreckage and moan their fate. A few get out and dig, as Sam Marble did. I supposed you were of that kind. What is the choice that you've really made, Neil?"

His choice? A few days ago, he, too, had thought of his life as a wagon that had broken down, yet he hadn't considered himself sunk in self-pity, one of those who sat in the wreckage and moaned. He had indeed strayed from the road on which he had first set out, the straight road that had its beginning in the Yellowstone Valley and was paved with values he'd thought to abandon. Now the fallacy of the choice he had made became clear to him, and the clarity came not so much from what Jenny had just said as from her example. Her wagon, too, had broken down, not once but many times. But she would indeed stand in the doorway, gun in hand, so that the paper could go to press.

He said slowly, "I'll go back over and tell Ogden that the *Bugle* is not for sale."

Ben Hare said, "Let him find out when

the paper is delivered to his door."

"No," Bowman said. "I'm thinking straight now. He must have no chance to run. He's got to answer for Miles."

"He's got company," Hare said, "Look."

He pointed through the window. A rider was swinging down from his saddle at the hitchrail before the Imperial, and that rider was Kemp Satterlee.

"Of course," said Bowman. "He's come to find out why Pete Beale didn't come back after being sent to Broken Wagon. Now I'll have both of them together."

Jenny said quickly, "Don't go, Neil! Satterlee will answer you with a gun!"

Bowman shook his head. "I'll have to risk it."

Ben Hare said, "Let him go, Jenny." Ben Hare understood.

Bowman moved to the door and stepped out. He heard Jenny call his name, but he didn't turn back. He had no words to explain to her what moved him now; he could not have told her of the dirt on his hands and the need he felt to rub the dirt away forever. He remembered Miles Hascomb lying grey and stricken in the stage station, yet this was no vengeance quest. He was done with vengeance.

He came across the planking and into

the sunlight of midstreet, and he was taking long strides when the fire bell began clanging in the tower, the sound beating hard against the morning quiet. That brass alarm penetrated through to Bowman, and he thought, Ogden! The *Bugle*! He turned, afraid that he'd see smoke rising from the rear of the newspaper plant; and mixed with that fear was the thought that he had underestimated Ogden.

CHAPTER SIXTEEN

Guns Speaking

Morning light had brought Jud Addison out of the deep sleep of one who'd drunk too much. Morosely he kicked the blankets off the jail cot and sat up. Now where the hell was he? Then full remembrance returned. No wonder his mouth tasted foul and a clamouring demand made him shaky. Some hair of the dog was what he needed. Or did he?

Damn, but he wished he could think straight! Whisky was no real friend, he told himself. Booze only riled him and magnified whatever happened to be eating on him, and then he did loco things. Like the several times he'd shot up the camp. The odd part of it was he really didn't care for the juice; it was just that he'd get feeling small and useless and he'd try making himself big by getting outside a lot of panther paint. Wasn't worth the price, though.

Afterwards he'd awake to the sickening realisation of what a fool he'd made of himself and how near he had come to doing something he'd regret the rest of his born days.

Last night, for instance.

He could remember prowling the camp looking for Bowman, every drink making more stabbing the thought of Helen in that man's arms in the warm, wild dark such as he himself had once known with her. Yet when he'd found Bowman and had a gun on him, he knew he hadn't really wanted to kill the man. Some deep-seated decency had whispered that whatever had happened between Bowman and Helen might have been not their fault entirely but something that had sprung from his own shortcomings. Hell, he'd as good as deserted her! And so he'd had his chance at Bowman and forfeited it, had lain blubbering on a saloon floor.

Two ways to look at anything, he guessed. What the hell was he doing, sitting here whitewashing Bowman when the man had moved into his house?

His house? Ah, there was the rub! It wasn't his house, not one nail of it; it never had been. And Helen wasn't his woman any more. How had they started straying apart? He reckoned it had begun when he'd brought her to Montana to a claim that petered out. Damn, but the chestiness had gone out of him then! On the way west he'd talked of a mansion in Butte, and maybe a string of racing horses such as bigwig Marcus Daly kept, but afterwards she'd slept in tents, in shacks where a mining king wouldn't have stabled a mule. Maybe he should have sent her back East till he'd made a stake. But he'd been a torn-apart man, seeing her fairness by lamplight and wanting her with him, yet seeing his own failure mirrored in her eyes.

Damn, if only they'd talked the whole thing out while there was still time. If only he had told her how hard it had hit him when she had the house built with money that had been none of his. Probably she hadn't meant to tear down his pride the way she had.

He arose from the cot and began pacing. He was roving the musty room when he heard his name called from beyond the window and recognised her voice.

He came to the window both eagerly and reluctantly. He opened it and grasped the bars, peering out upon Placer Street. He saw Helen standing there, fair and handsome in the morning. All his love for her crowded his throat, yet he kept his face still and his eyes remote; this was his ingrained habit of defence. She was wearing her best dress, purple silk cut to a style nearly a decade gone, with a cameo brooch, a family heirloom, fastened to the collar. She wore pearl eardrops that had been her mother's. Looking at her, he was acutely conscious of his own rumpled, sour-smelling condition.

"Helen," he asked, "did you have to come here?"

"Yes, Jud," she said. "To tell you I'm ready to go away with you."

He shook his head, not believing. "You'd clear out of this camp?"

"We've had no luck here, Jud. The stage leaves for Helena towards noon. I've cash enough to buy two tickets. We can board up the house or rent it to someone. Shall I ask Sam Marble to turn you loose?"

Again he shook his head, and memories came crowding in fitful flashes — the little girl in the house on the Illinois hill, when he'd been a boy looking upwards — the stuffy parlour where her disapproving parents had dourly watched them being married — all the joys of that trip west — all the bitterness that had followed. He'd asked too much. That was it. He'd asked her to give up the ease she'd been born to, so that she might follow his ill-fated star.

He gripped the bars tightly and said, "No more tents, no more shacks. Not for you, Helen."

Her lips trembled, and her composure nearly left her. "Last night a man pointed the way for me. You hate him, but he's proved to be our best friend, yours and mine. He said I'd have to make a choice. It's you or the house on the slope, isn't it, Jud? I've made my choice."

"No," he said, more firmly, "It wouldn't work. Like Lot's wife, after Sodom, you'd always be looking back. In every shack we bunked in, you'd be remembering. I'd know, and I'd turn to the bottle again. And some day you'd buy *one* stage ticket. To bring you back here."

"You're sure of that, Jud?"

"Certain sure."

"And no words of mine will persuade you?"

"The house is bigger than anything you can say."

She turned away. He watched the proud set of her back and thought that her shoulders shook. He swung about, not wanting to see. He sat down on the cot and buried his face in his hands.

He sat for a long, long time, conscious of nothing but his own misery. Then a key scratched in a padlock. The door of this old cabin now being used as a jail swung inwards and Sam Marble stood there.

The old prospector was carrying a tray. This he brought over and placed upon the end of the cot. A funny geezer, Sam, with his tangled whiskers and his fancy waistcoat, Jud thought. In a voice as hearty as Kris Kringle's, Marble said, "Danged near forgot we had somebody jailed. I brought you a good breakfast, Jud. Best I could buy."

Addison said, "You can let me out of this trap, Sam. I'm sober now."

Marble didn't look squarely at him. "Not to-day, Jud."

"Why not?"

Marble moved back towards the door. He put himself against the wall and made an aimless motion with his hands, and it struck Addison that the man was highly embarrassed. Sam had been too hearty, coming in. Addison asked again, "Why not?"

Marble said, "I'm old enough to know men. I've pegged you for a good one, not near so wild as you make out. I wouldn't want you in bad trouble, Jud."

"Turn me loose and I'm gone from this camp. As far as I can get."

Marble had the sick look of a kindly man faced with a mean job. "I didn't aim to tell you, Jud. Ain't many minutes ago Sig Ogden sent word to me by his swamper. Seems Bowman is willing to sell Sig his interest in the paper. But the price is stiff, so Sig wanted to borrow a few thousand from me. I went straight to the stage depot to weigh out dust I keep in the Wells Fargo safe. Your wife was there. Buying two stage tickets."

Addison stared. "Then she must have gone from here to the depot. We quarrelled, Sam. She spoke about a choice, but she didn't tell me what other choice she might make. One ticket for her, one for Bowman."

Marble said, "That's how I figgered it, knowing that Bowman is selling out. And that's why I've got to keep you locked up a while. I don't want you doing murder before that stage leaves."

He slipped through the doorway and quickly snapped the padlock into place. Addison stared at the door. He supposed he should be fighting mad, but instead he was only sick deep inside. He had lost Helen beyond any recall; he could see that now. He stared at the breakfast tray and had no appetite. He merely sat, all his thoughts bleak. After a while he heard the fire bell suddenly fill the morning. It was like a death knell, only faster — beating, beating, beating. Hell, the whole camp could burn for all he cared!

Still, he got up and moved to the window. He could see a good part of Placer Street, and standing in the middle of the street was Neil Bowman. He looked above Bowman, above the false front of the Imperial, his gaze drawn up the north slope where a spiral of smoke rose from the big house there. Helen's house! It took him a moment to realise who had fired it. And why.

Fascinated, he stared at the mushrooming smoke and saw the first flicker of flame. She must have used plenty of coal oil, outside and in. He went down to his knees and again pressed his hands to his face. Shuddering shook him mightily; mingled in him with humility and joy with the full awareness of the sacrifice she had made for him. . . .

Bowman, stopped in midstreet by the fire bell, stared back at the *Bugle* plant, his eyes searching for what he feared to see.

261

No smoke was there but the chimney's smoke. He shook his head, not understanding. The bell was drawing people from everywhere; they spilled from doorways and thronged the streets. Voices babbled and questions flew back and forth. Then someone who'd reached a vantage point between two buildings where the upper north slope could be glimpsed, shouted, "Addisons' place!" Bowman looked and saw the smoke rising.

He was almost ashamed of the sense of relief that swept through him with the certainty that the *Bugle* had not been fired. He remembered seeing Helen Addison on the street when he'd come out of the Imperial a while ago. The thought of her gave him a new fear. Was she trapped up there? But clearly to him came her voice out of last night saying, "I know now what I'm going to do," and remembering that, he knew what she had done. In his mind, Bowman saluted her.

Men were swarming along the planking. Some, bearing buckets, were running hard. They were of a volunteer brigade, he supposed. They would do what could be done.

He walked on towards the Imperial. Men buffeted him in passing, and he almost had to fight his way across the planking before the saloon. He got inside and found Faro still seated at his table. Here, it appeared, was the one man in Broken Wagon who'd not been pulled by curiosity or alarm at the fire bell's ringing.

Faro looked up but did not seem to see him. Faro's eyes were blank, looking only inward.

Bowman walked to the middle of the barroom. "Ogden!" he shouted. "Come down here!"

He saw then that he'd had no need to call. Ogden and Satterlee were both on the landing above, drawn, doubtless, by the fire bell. Ogden was already starting down the stairs. He got halfway and stopped, his eyes fixed on Bowman. Satterlee still stood above, big and blocky.

"The deal's off," Bowman said. "I'm not selling, Sig."

Ogden said, "But I'll meet the price. I've already made arrangements to raise the whole sum."

"No deal," Bowman said. "There's Hascomb to think about. Money won't pay for him. You'll go to the Miners' Council, both of you, and own up to his death and that drifter's."

Something flickered across Ogden's face that was wicked to see. He said in a low voice, "What manner of fool do you take me for?"

Faro spoke up. "You'll deal me cards in this. For nearly an hour I've been here steeling myself to do what must be done. I'm not going to be cheated of my chance."

Bowman saw the gun then, the gun Faro had placed on the table before him. No tiny sneak gun of the man's profession, but over two pounds of single action .45 Peacemaker.

Bowman said quickly, "Faro, this is my affair."

"No," Faro said. "He only tried to kill you. I'm the one who was to live, but strictly on his terms. Killing a soul is a greater crime than killing a man. Ever since the Twosleep, I've known what I must do. Now I'm ready."

Bowman said, "I'm here for Hascomb. I hoped there wouldn't be a fight."

Satterlee had taken a spread-legged stand, and his broad face had brightened with anger. "The hell with talk," he said and brought his gun out.

Bowman found no time for reluctance. He met Satterlee's movement with one of his own, bringing his gun up and out of its holster and hearing its explosion with surprise. Too loud, that roar. Then he realised that Faro had fired at the same time. Satterlee turned fully around. Bowman had a quick glimpse of Ogden with a gun out and poised; the man seemed frozen. Satterlee went somersaulting down the stairs, his crashing body sweeping Ogden's legs out from under him. The two hit the floor in a shapeless tangle. Bowman moved forward carefully, his gun held ready. He nudged Ogden with his boot toe and then reached down with his free hand and turned the man over and saw that he was dead.

"My bullet, I believe," Faro said in a calm voice and put the Peacemaker back on the table. "Sig was dead before Satterlee spilled him." Faro stood up, looking immensely tall. "I once charged you with not having proved yourself, Bowman. Ironic that we should both have been tested together."

Bowman felt sick. He had not wanted bloodshed, realising that blood was no more easily wiped from a man's hand than dirt. He looked down at the two on the floor and found no good in this moment. He had never killed a man before; he hoped he would never kill another.

Or would he? There was Bart Carney

265

waiting, but there would be no money for Carney. That money belonged to others. He, Bowman, would return the money to the law. This was a swift decision strangely come by until he thought about it. He had just made amends for Miles Hascomb, but he'd done more than that. When he walked into this place, he'd come back to his own beginnings, back to the values he had abandoned in bitterness behind Deer Lodge's walls. And he had to be fully one man or the other; he knew that now.

He walked out of the Imperial. The fire bell no longer beat out its brass alarm, and the street no longer swarmed. People now gathered in knots, their faces lifted towards the slope where the smoke rose, but some were staring curiously towards the Imperial. They'd heard the wall-muffled shots, he supposed.

Sam Marble came running down the street, his arms flailing. He gestured towards the slope. "No chance of stopping the fire," he shouted. "The house is gone for sure."

Bowman stepped towards him and held up his hand for Marble to slow down. Bowman inclined his head towards the saloon. "Ogden and Satterlee are dead in there. They were partners. To-day's *Bugle* will tell you all about it."

Marble looked like a man to whom too much had happened in too short a time. "Sig and Kemp — partners?" He raised his hands and let them drop. "Trouble always tramps close behind you, Bowman. First Jud, and now this. I'm of a mind to lock you up."

Faro had come out of the Imperial and taken a stand behind Bowman. Faro said, "No, Sam. I can vouch for this man. He's one of us."

Marble shook his head. "I'm going somewhere and get me a big drink."

Bowman said softly, "Helen —"

She had come down off the slope and was walking Placer, heading towards them. She had a shawl over her shoulders, and a small carpetbag in one hand. She walked like a queen, head up and face serene. She came swiftly yet with dignity; and when she reached them, she turned to Sam Marble. "I want you to know that I am the person who fired my house," she said.

"But why, ma'am?" he demanded. "Why?"

"To prove that the house was not really important," she said. "There's no wind blowing this morning and no other house close to mine, so there was no danger of

267

the fire's spreading. And now, if you'll release my husband, we have tickets on the stage out of here."

Marble was a man too bewildered for words. He passed a hand before his eyes; he shook his head again. "Come along," he said and started towards the jail building.

Helen Addison passed Bowman with a swish of her skirts; she looked at him and thanked him with her eyes, her smile both sad and happy.

Bowman watched her walk across the street, and Ruth's words came to him: "Whither thou goest, I will go; and where thou lodgest, I will lodge —"

Stepping off the planking, he started over to the *Bugle*'s plant.

CHAPTER SEVENTEEN

Man and Maid

Jenny awaited him as he came into the office, and he was struck by the look she wore. She stood with her eyes liquid and warm, a great happiness showing on her, but the shadow of worry still lingered as though she did not yet fully believe that he had come back unscathed. Not till now did he realise how it had been for her since he'd walked from this room. The waiting had been harder than the doing; and this was his reward, seeing her glad at his return.

How had they drawn so close to each other in so short a time? He remembered the Twosleep and the fire they'd shared; he remembered how she had waited through the night at Circle 6 and waited again yesterday, knowing that Jud Addison was prowling the town for him. Man and maid, they had known loneliness, each in a different way, and they had shared danger in a common cause. Time had so little to do with the things that drew two people together.

"I watched from the window," she said. "When the fire bell rang, I saw you look this way. I hoped you might come back. Then I watched till you came out of the Imperial. I thought I heard shots. Is everything all right?"

"Yes," he said. He'd have to tell her later what had happened. Now there was a last thing left to be done. A thing he'd have to force himself to do quickly before he wavered in the attempt. Damn, but it wasn't easy to give up all of his old notion!

He said, "I'd like the five thousand dollars I gave you. It wasn't mine to spend. If Ben told you about my prison record, he probably also told you his suspicion of how I came to have the money."

"He told me," she said.

From the back room came the rumble of the press; Ben Hare was putting out the edition. Faro, then, had not been the only person immune to the excitement of the fire. Bowman watched Jenny go to the roll-top desk and rummage beneath some papers in a drawer. She brought forth the bundle of currency and placed it in his hands. He stowed the money in the saddlebag. Then he took a pen and hastily scribbled a note which began: "To whom it may concern." He put the note in with the money and strapped the bag tightly. He picked up the bag and started towards the door.

Jenny said, "You'll come back, Neil?"

"I don't know," he said, and he was thinking of Bart Carney. He walked to Jenny and kissed her cheek. "I hope so," he said. "Soon."

She raised her hand to her cheek and asked incongruously, "You didn't lose anything in the fire?"

"No," he said. "I lost nothing in that house."

He went out and strode towards the stage station. Up on the north slope, the Addison house still blazed, and people milled about the place, restless figures on the hillside. Others still gathered on the street, watching. He wondered how far the news of Ogden's death had spread; and remembering how the livery stable hostler had felt about Ogden, he braced himself for the camp's animosity. The hell with them! Satterlee had died with Ogden. That should tell the people half the story; the *Bugle* would tell the rest.

No man scowled at him as he walked

along. Well, he had done something for Broken Wagon as well as for himself when he'd braced that pair in the Imperial; and thinking that, he began warming to the camp's people. How many days ago had it been that he'd felt no kinship as he had eaten alone, a stranger? He supposed he'd scorned those about him because he could not afford friendliness. He shook his head. He could see now how futile and costly had been the tough philosophy he'd once imagined was his.

At the station, the stage was loading for Helena. The old driver waved to him from the railed-in roof where he was stowing luggage. The driver was another with whom he had shared danger, and so they were friends.

Bowman heaved the saddlebag up to him. "Turn this over to a federal marshal or the county sheriff when you get to Helena," he said. There, damn it, it was done!

"Sure," the driver said. He grinned. "No more Indian scare to worry about. Word came over the wire this morning that the soldiers had a little skirmish and Sword-Bearer got himself shot. Nearly all the Indians have gone back to the agency. Some of them redskins figger Sword-

Bearer will bring himself alive again. But his magic sword sure as hell didn't work."

Bowman shook his head, feeling a loss that was queerly personal. Sword-Bearer, like himself, had put his feet on a hopeless path, and Sword-Bearer had died for his mistake. Come to think of it, Sword-Bearer had had an indirect hand in Neil Bowman's destiny. If there had been no Indian scare there would have been no murder at the change station, and he wouldn't have tarried in Broken Wagon. The strings got pulled, and the people danced, each in his own fashion.

Helen and Jud Addison were standing in the stage depot doorway. Bowman saw them as he turned away from the coach. He tipped his hat to the woman and would have walked on, but Jud called out, "Just a minute." He left the doorway and came towards Bowman, a big, bearded man, awkward and embarrassed. It was plain that he had something to say but was hard put for words. He thrust out his hand to Bowman and said, "How big a fool can a man make of himself in one lifetime?"

Bowman took his hand. "I don't know," he said. "I haven't lived that long. I wish you luck in Helena."

"I was there a week ago," Addison said.

"Man offered me a job with a freighting line. Think I'll take it. I can't get rich fast, so I'll try getting rich slow."

"You're already rich," Bowman said. He smiled at Helen and touched his hat again and walked on.

He came to the livery stable and got his horse and rode out of Broken Wagon.

Now to finish it, he thought.

He followed the stage road, but only till it took him beyond Placer and into the timber that pressed close against this end of camp. He picked a careful way through the trees in a wide arc calculated to bring him behind that deserted cabin where Bart Carney waited. Out here in the timber, he might have been deep in the wilderness; but clearly to him came the sounds of the town, amplified by the high, thin air of the mountain country — the call of one man to another, the shrill laughter of a woman, the creaking of a pulley over a well. He was no more than a hundred yards from the road, and he heard the stage clatter by.

Dismounting, he tied his horse to a bush and worked forward on foot. He came to the rear of a cabin so old that he knew it had been here long before Broken Wagon had sprung up. A sagging lean-to was tacked to the building; and when he peered inside, he found a saddled horse patiently standing. He recognised the brand and remembered the meal he'd had at Muleshoe on his way up to the buried loot. The horse swung its head and regarded him.

Bowman backed away. The cabin had a rear window, but the glass was long since gone. He crept to the window and crouched down and got out his gun and held it ready. Then he removed his hat and lifted his eyes over the ledge. He saw a room that held only the backless wreckage of a chair; he looked across the room to the open front door which hung upon one leather hinge, and in the instant that he realised the room was empty, he knew he'd forgotten how wary a wolf can be.

Carney's voice drove at him, cold and harsh. "Drop that gun, boy!"

He let the gun slip from his fingers. He came up from his crouched position and turned slowly and saw Carney standing at a corner of the lean-to. Carney had been hiding in the woods close by. Carney held a gun at hip level, and his face was taut with anger. "So it's bounty money you're figuring on now, Neil," he said. "I gave you a chance last night, and this is what I get for it." His anger blazed to full fury.

"Damned if I'm not going to pistol-whip you within an inch of your life!"

"Now wait a minute, Bart!"

But Carney was coming at him with gun upraised. Bowman threw up his arms and took the shock of a blow on his left forearm. Anger had now stripped Carney of caution, and Bowman got his fingers around the man's right wrist. At the same time he kicked Carney's legs out from under him. The two of them went down in a tangle and writhed upon the ground, rolling, grunting, and clawing at each other. It was a silent fight, silent as that one the first night they'd been cell-mates, but it was a tougher fight, for anger had strengthened Carney. The breath was sobbing in Bowman's throat before he got Carney under him and could hold him there. He put his knees on Carney's shoulders, pinning them down, and he twisted the gun from Carney's hand and tossed it aside.

"Now, damn it, listen to me!" Bowman panted.

Carney cursed him.

"Bart, I got my gun out only to be sure you'd listen. I'd come to tell you that I got the money back this morning, but it's not for you. Or for me either. I've sent it to the law."

Carney twisted beneath him. "What kind of a sandy you trying to run now?"

"No sandy. The money's on its way to Helena."

"You're talking straight?"

"Straight as a string, Bart."

"Why did you do it?"

"Because the money was never any damn' good to me, and it wouldn't have been any good to you. You'd have spent it fast and remembered how easy it came and you'd have gone out to get more the same way. Sooner or later it would have put you back in Deer Lodge, or some other pen."

Carney quit his struggling. He lay there staring up at Bowman, searching his face, and then the anger slowly died in Carney's eyes. "You've learned young," Carney said at last. "You've learned what it took me nearly thirty years to catch on to. I decided last night to teach you the lesson, boy. I wanted you to learn that you can't easy get something that isn't yours. But then you had to show up here with a gun in your fist. What the hell was I to think? You can get off my brisket now."

But Bowman hesitated. "You won't jump me if I do?"

Carney said, "I've been turning things over in my mind ever since I found that

277

empty hole. Maybe like you last night, I'm tired of fighting, tired of running." He grinned. "Mexico's a long way off, but there's Canada. There must be one ranch in Alberta that can use a hand and no questions asked." He looked hard at Bowman, laughter wrinkles deep-etched at the corners of his eyes. "Unless you've got so damned law-abiding, boy, that nothing short of seeing me back in Deer Lodge will keep you off my trail."

Bowman grinned, too. "You told me once that the Territory was willing to make a dicker — a shorter sentence if you'd lead them to your loot." He got to his feet and extended a hand and helped Carney up. "Well, they're getting their pound of cash and you've paid your pound of time. Six years, wasn't it? Just keep an eye peeled for sunlight shining on tin stars till you're across the border, Bart."

"Hell," Carney said. "Maybe you pounded some sense into me just now, but I don't need any barrel of advice from a sprout like you."

Bowman picked up Carney's gun and handed it to him. "Good luck, Bart."

Carney said, "There may come a time when I'll reach in my pocket and find it empty, and I'll remember what a damn' fool I was to let that loot get away from me. There may come a time when you'll read about me in the papers again. Try to think kindly of me, if you do. I can make the climb, but I ain't sure I can perch overlong in that top bunk."

He cased his gun, turned his back to Bowman, and stepped into the lean-to. Bowman picked up his own gun and hat and walked back through the trees to his horse. When he'd risen to saddle, he shook his head and said, unbelievingly, "The old hellion!" He wasn't sure whether he'd just taught Bart a lesson or learned one from him. Still, he supposed Bart was the wisest man he'd ever known. But, no, there was Miles Hascomb, who, dying, had seen deep into the heart of another man. Deeper than he had seen into himself that night, Bowman reflected. Now how had Miles Hascomb guessed he might win his gamble?

Bowman rode back to camp past the livery stable and past the restaurant where he'd taken his meals. He saw Faro striding along, his shoulders square, and he judged that wherever Faro now walked, he would walk with honour. He came to the jail building and thought of Jud Addison on the road to Helena and hope. He looked at the Imperial across the way and remembered that he'd told Jenny that to-morrow, next week, or next month another Ogden would roll into camp with another quick-money scheme. So be it. He'd find the strength for any fight that would have to be made. And to-morrow or next week a man might arrive who would complete Ogden's packing plant and run it honestly. Or maybe the miners would take over the task. He could hear the hammers still beating up there on the slope.

On the opposite hillside, smoke lazily lifted; the Addison place was a jackstraw heap of fallen, smouldering timbers, and the bucket brigade had dispersed. He lighted down before the *Bugle* office and left the roan with reins trailing. He came inside, and Jenny rose from her chair to meet him.

"I'm back," he said and smiled, realising how pointless that sounded.

He was at once aware that the press had gone silent, and this troubled him. He looked towards the doorway leading to the other room. Jenny must have understood, for she said, "Ben's gone for his morning drink. He'll get the paper out; you can be sure of that."

"I'll tend to it," he said. "Provided you'd

like to hire another pressman."

She smiled; the smile made her girlish and bright and carefree. "Have you forgotten? You're a partner in this establishment."

"No," he said. "Not any more. But I could use a job here, Jenny." He fumbled in his pocket for the agreement that had been drawn between him and Miles Hascomb and laid it carefully on the table. "I forgot to return this when you gave me back the money."

She picked up the sheet of notebook paper, then let it fall. "Faro told me the approximate wording. I see he remembered well. It mentions a dollar and other valuable considerations. I know all about the valuable considerations. Have you got a dollar, Neil?"

He searched his pockets. "I'm afraid not," he said. "I spent the last of my own money this morning for breakfast." Suddenly he threw back his head and laughed in pure joyousness. He couldn't remember how long it had been since he'd laughed like that; certainly he'd not felt so carefree since that day in court. Then he sobered, remembering what Bart Carney had said about a man's not easily getting something that wasn't his. "No, Jenny. I'll be a hired hand till I've earned enough to buy a piece of this plant." He took off his coat and threw it upon the table and started towards the press room. "There's work to be done," he said.

Jenny shook her head. "Need you be in such a tearing hurry, Neil?"

He turned towards her and saw that a new mood had caught her; she was solemn from something this moment held, but it was a warm solemnity, with its own kind of promise. Looking at her, he remembered how at their first meeting he'd judged her to be harder than the rocks of these hills. He remembered, too, her indifference and knew that it had been a pose, born from all the hard days she had known, her only guard against further disappointments. All along she had needed someone to shield her. Now they were together. All their days would hold giving and taking, but he was the one who would always be indebted, for it was her wisdom that had shown him the way. Let the wagon break down a hundred times, the lesson was forever learned.

He held open his arms, and she moved towards him, smiling. . . .

The employees of Thorndike Press hope you have enjoyed this Large Print book. All our Large Print titles are designed for easy reading, and all our books are made to last. Other Thorndike Press Large Print books are available at your library, through selected bookstores, or directly from the publisher.

For more information about titles, please call:

(800) 223-1244
(800) 223-6121

To share your comments, please write:

Publisher
Thorndike Press
P.O. Box 159
Thorndike, Maine 04986